Love is
a time of enchantment:
in it all days are fair and all fields
green. Youth is blest by it,
old age made benign:
the eyes of love see
roses blooming in December,
and sunshine through rain. Verily
is the time of true-love
a time of enchantment — and
Oh! how eager is woman
to be bewitched!

# THE LYDEARD BEAUTY

Susan Gillow meets her perfect hero when Jermyn, her distant and hitherto unknown cousin, comes to stay at Reibridge Place. However, she discovers that her recently-widowed mama has marriage plans of her own with another of their house-guests: Lord John Deville, one of Regency London's most eligible bachelors. Susan is dismayed at the prospect of Lord John as a stepfather, for he does all in his power to prevent her relationship with Jermyn prospering.

Books by Audrey Blanshard
in the Ulverscroft Large Print Series:

THE SHY YOUNG DENBURY
GRANBOROUGH'S FILLY
THE FRENSHAM INHERITANCE
A VIRGINIAN AT VENNCOMBE

AUDREY BLANSHARD

# THE
# LYDEARD
# BEAUTY

*Complete and Unabridged*

# ULVERSCROFT
*Leicester*

First published in Great Britain in 1979 by
Robert Hale Limited
London

First Large Print Edition
published March 1994
by arrangement with
Robert Hale Limited
London

British Library CIP Data

Blanshard, Audrey
The Lydeard beauty.—Large print ed.—
Ulverscroft large print series: romance
I. Title
823.914 [F]

ISBN 0–7089–3037–9

Published by
F. A. Thorpe (Publishing) Ltd.
Anstey, Leicestershire
Set by Words & Graphics Ltd.
Anstey, Leicestershire
Printed and bound in Great Britain by
T. J. Press (Padstow) Ltd., Padstow, Cornwall

This book is printed on acid-free paper

# 1

"LA, sir, I had not thought to see *you* here! I vow you must detest these fashionable squeezes quite as much as I do!" Thus the Hon. Lavinia Lightfoot addressed the dashing Lord Quantock at Lady Spindleberry's drum.

His lordship smiled agreeably and said —

At this point the ink on Miss Gillow's pen ran dry and with it her rapid flow of words. The ink was easily replenished from the fine silver standish on the library table; not so her narrative — or more precisely, her dialogue.

Staring out unseeingly through the window at the autumn-tinted parkland of her home, Reibridge Place, she wondered if the ton really used such words as 'La!' and 'Fie!' half a century ago. Indeed, she had sampled so little of fashionable life herself that she scarcely knew which expressions were the current vogue. Her source for such matters came entirely from novels and one or two plays, which had on occasion been read for the performance of home theatricals. She could consult her mama but, although as an accredited Beauty in her youth she had moved in the highest circles of society, she was barely seven-and-thirty even now. Susan did a quick calculation in the corner of the paper before the ink should dry again: no, her parent's memory would certainly not extend reliably before the 1790's.

Besides, how her mama — who had never so much as read a novel — would stare if she discovered the reason for her enquiries! Of grandparents Susan had none, so there was really nowhere she could turn for enlightenment on these teasing matters.

Resolving to abandon any niceties of style she applied herself again to the dashing Lord Quantock's reply . . .

It was no use, his lordship maintained a stubborn silence, and in fifteen minutes Susan found herself quite rigid with boredom — a condition which writing her first novel had been supposed to dispel.

Perhaps her scheme was over-ambitious; after all, nearly every fashionable novel she had read was a *roman à clef*, and at eighteen her experience of life was scarcely sufficient to encompass a true tale of passion and high drama — even at second-hand, she thought gloomily. By placing the story firmly back in the last century she had hoped to fire her imagination, but it was plainly going to do nothing of the sort.

As far as she had been able to discover not a breath of scandal had ever touched the Gillow family, so there was nothing there she could turn to good account. The least one would expect, with a famous Beauty as a parent, was a history of ill-starred amours and broken-hearted — even brangling beaux; but her mama, Aurelia Lydeard, had apparently dazzled the world for a year after her come-out, then married Sir Henry Gillow, a widower with a seven year old son, without a murmur and lived happily ever since.

Until, that is, six months ago when

Sir Henry had been killed suddenly, leaving a deeply grieving widow and family behind him.

The lambent blue eyes, the fine almost translucent complexion, and rich corn-coloured hair of the Lydeard Beauty were all undimmed by the passage of the years — everybody said so, and it was in any event perfectly clear from her likeness taken at seventeen; even the faultless sylph-like form had been miraculously preserved in spite of bearing Sir Henry two sons and three daughters. But what time had failed to achieve mourning had now accomplished; her mama's beauty was hidden from the world by a widow's weeds and seclusion.

Susan fetched a deep sigh, mostly of annoyance. The whole point of writing a book had been to banish these morose reflections for a while, and here she was going over the unhappy business yet again. If papa hadn't fallen from his horse on the last day of the hunting season, she would have been presented in the spring — it had all been arranged. Who could tell what might have happened by now?

A cavalcade of missed balls and

assemblies passed before her mind's eye — each occasion more brilliant than the last; and her partners, of course, were unequalled in looks, wit and address. In reality the summer had produced just three invitations to dinner at houses in the immediate vicinity, two picnics (one wet), and a solitary tongue-tied admirer in the form of Timothy Etheridge, the squire's son.

She jabbed the pen crossly in the ink and resolved once more that Lord Quantock should say *something* agreeably —

"Oh, drat it!"

Susan scowled at the ruffle of deep lavender lace at her wrist, now spotted with ink.

"Really, my dear, such intemperate language in a House of Mourning."

Susan turned and transferred the scowl briefly to the speaker, Aunt Selworthy, papa's long-widowed sister, a lady whose gently moaning nature had for the past ten years fitted her bereavement like a glove.

"I was not aware anyone was there," Susan explained rather shortly, "but look what has happened!" She held out her hand to display the blotched trimming.

"Oh, dreadful — quite ruined, and it was such a pretty dress . . . It will never wash out, you know."

"Well, if it does not, it will be simple enough to replace the ruffle," Susan countered in brisk tones, as always meeting her aunt's gloom with a brightness she often did not feel.

"I suppose it may," Mrs Selworthy agreed, "although perhaps it will not be worth it."

"But the dress is almost new!" Susan protested.

"Indeed it is — made expressly for your mourning," her aunt said, more morosely than ever. "However, your mama is putting off her blacks now, I collect, and one supposes the rest of us must follow suit," she concluded in aggrieved tones.

Susan was mildly surprised. "I had thought mama intended a full year's second-mourning."

She cast her literary efforts face down to prevent her aunt seeing them with her sharp eyes: however it was too late.

6

"I trust you are not writing *clandestinely* to a beau," that lady said in all seriousness.

"Would that I were!" exclaimed Susan ruefully, and unable to resist quizzing her aunt, who could be relied upon never to see the humorous side of anything. "But what is this about mama abandoning her mourning?" she asked as a diversion whilst she gathered up her papers in a casual fashion.

Agnes Selworthy was not wholly satisfied with this response but was easily tempted into returning to her original grievance. She drew herself up to her full, if inconsiderable height and tucked in her chin, making herself look even plumper in the face than she was.

"Aurelia tells me she has quite made up her mind to throw the house open to visitors once again and resume her social life to the full."

Susan rose and was seen to be several inches taller than her aunt; and her dress of lavender and black striped sarsenet and slim shape were in sharp contrast with the sepulchral and squab form of her relative. Thick lustrous hair was the only dark feature of the girl and, with its healthy gloss, in no way imparted a dismal aspect to her appearance.

"Oh, capital!" Her pale blue eyes — the one feature of her mother's beauty she had inherited — shone with anticipation, but before she had the opportunity to say another word Mrs Selworthy continued repressively:

"It is not being done for your benefit, miss, that much I do know. No, Aurelia thinks Edwin should have his sporting friends about him during the winter months." The corners of her mouth were pulled down in disapproval, rendering her the perfect picture of a sulky infant — or so her niece thought. "So she says, but she can't humbug me," she hinted darkly.

"I cannot imagine what you mean by that," Susan retorted in quite sharp tones. "It seems perfectly reasonable that Edwin should want some companionship for his shooting and hunting. You make it sound as though mama is planning to hold a Paphian debauch at Reibridge!" She was instantly contrite, but there was something about her lugubrious

8

aunt which invariably goaded her into such outrageous remarks. "Oh, I'm sorry — really I am!"

"Very well," Mrs Selworthy said, accepting the apology with as much dignity as she could muster amidst her girlish blushes. "But you must endeavour to curb that wayward tongue of yours, or it will lead you into *terrible trouble*." After an almost imperceptible pause for this stricture to sink in, she went on: "Your mama has already made up her list of guests for the first house-party."

"When is it to be, then? She has said nothing of this to me."

"No, well, it was an impetuous and possibly ill-judged resolve in my view, but we'll say no more upon that head," she declared in accents of the utmost self-control. "It is fixed for the end of the month. Henry's old friends are invited, which is as it should be — and the Davenports, the Mainwarings, Major Welton . . . Oh, together with a number of gentlemen whose names escape me now. And," she paused ominously, "Lord John Deville."

Which was *not* as it should be,

concluded Susan, but as she had never heard of the gentleman the inference was quite lost upon her. However, it all sounded very promising.

"Deville? I don't believe I know him."

"I should hope not, indeed." Mrs Selworthy shook her head, making the black ribbons on her cap dance briefly about. "I fear your poor mama has run mad, my dear. But there, it is not to be wondered at after such shock and grief, I suppose." She squeezed out a sympathetic tear and, apparently too moved to utter another word, left in a flurry of bombazine and crape.

Sir Edwin, Susan's half-brother, almost collided with the overwrought lady as he stepped into the library.

He raised an interrogatory eyebrow. "And what's amiss with Aunt Sniffworthy now?" he asked Susan as he walked in an aimless fashion over to the window.

"You are at the root of her discontent, I collect," she told him mischievously.

"I? Why, I scarcely ever set eyes upon the complaining old trout." This response lacked the bantering tone which would have softened his remark and rendered

10

it more acceptable.

Susan, still clasping her papers, studied thoughtfully the straight-backed figure clad in dress — a little over-elegant for the country — of tailcoat, Wellington trousers and shoes; she wondered if Edwin would ever regain his carefree manner.

The casual observer would naturally attribute his change of character to the recent death of his father, and the subsequent assumption of the title and all the responsibilities which accompanied it. Susan knew it was not so. The alteration had been apparent to her when he had returned from Brussels and the battlefield at Waterloo over a year before. Lieutenant Gillow sustained no physical injury during the action but the effect upon him had been profound, nonetheless. At five-and-twenty it had been his first engagement on the field of battle, and he had sold out soon afterwards.

Susan, at eighteen, and the eldest child of Sir Henry's second marriage, had always felt closer to her half-brother than to the rest of the family — in spite of the eight year gap between them

— because her four younger brothers and sisters were even now under fifteen years of age and still virtually children. They both shared the dark-haired, well-defined features of their father and were more alike than many a full brother and sister. But even Susan was unable to coax Edwin out of the sullens these days.

"No, it is really mama who has outraged her by having the audacity to invite a few people for a house-party two weeks from now — and we are to put off our blacks at least."

"I am glad to hear that," said Sir Edwin with some feeling: he found the mourning state irksome in the extreme and a decided check upon his taste for modish dress. "But why am I to shoulder the blame — or indeed the credit — for it?"

"Oh, merely because it will be a gathering of your sporting cronies," Susan assured him.

He turned from contemplation of the extensive acres of parkland, whose recent possession seemed to have afforded him

12

so little pleasure, and looked at his half-sister with a shade more interest in his dark eyes.

"Who is to be invited, then? I suppose mama has had the making up of the list?" He sounded disgruntled.

"Why yes, of course she has! Who else could have the ordering of such matters?" she asked in puzzled tones.

"You could, Suke," he countered promptly. "It is quite the thing these days for the eldest girl to take the lead, especially in town."

Susan gave a short laugh. "You appear to be forgetting that although I may be the eldest I have not yet been presented, let alone be in a position to usurp mama's duties! Besides, mama is far from being the decrepit widow. In fact she is really not *old* at all."

"No, she is astonishingly youthful-looking still, I grant you that, but I daresay the guests won't be! More papa's cronies than mine, I'll wager."

"Well, in the main, yes," Susan conceded. "But your friend Major Welton was mentioned, and I daresay there are more. Aunt Selworthy couldn't remember

13

them all. However, you have only to say and mama will invite anyone you propose, you know that."

"True. I will have a word with her when — "

"By the by," Susan cut across him, "is Lord John Deville one of your acquaintance?"

Sir Edwin frowned. "Why do you ask? He isn't invited, is he?"

"Oh, but he is." Susan watched him closely. "Isn't he fit for polite society, or something? Aunt Selworthy behaved as if he were the devil himself."

Permitting himself a wry smile, Sir Edwin said a little more easily:

"I can imagine the gentleman would not be first oars with her, although how he has been brought to her notice at all I cannot apprehend." Then in disinterested tones he added: "He is the second son of the old Duke of Anlaby — a real out and outer and Man of the Town. As rich as Golden Ball even though he ain't the heir."

Susan thought she detected a hint of envy in the last remark, but soon dismissed this: how could a mere baronet's

14

heir expect to be as wealthy as a duke's son?

"How old is this fascinating gentleman?" she pursued.

Sir Edwin pondered briefly. "Mid-thirties or thereabouts, but he has remained utterly impervious to the charms of every eligible young lady put in his way, so you need entertain no hopes on *that* head, Suke. He is, after all, the same age as mama."

Their eyes met in a moment of shared perception, and Susan murmured: "Is that why Aunt Selworthy disapproves so violently — she thinks mama is husband-hunting so soon! Why, it's preposterous! As if she would!"

"Is it?" Sir Edwin said mildly. "That is not to say the old croaker is right in this case, but I think we must not be too surprised if we acquire a stepfather eventually. Mama is still a very attractive woman — as much a Beauty as she always was, in many ways."

"Yes, it's true, she is," admitted Susan, who always found it a sore trial being the Lydeard Beauty's daughter: comparisons were as unflattering as they

15

were inevitable. "But I cannot believe it, all the same," she maintained stoutly. "I don't say she will *never* re-marry, but to be casting out lures at the first company we entertain after papa's death — no, it is not to be thought of." She was anxious to attend to her fast-drying ink-stains now, and was about to take her leave, but said first: "Did you come to the library for any particular purpose? I fear I diverted you with this house-party nonsense."

There was an air of abstraction about him, and he started a little at her question. "No — well, yes. I am looking for one of papa's account books. Heasley maintains there is at least one missing, and everything has to be point-device for that gentleman, I am discovering ... I must go up to town to see him again soon," he put in, almost as an after-thought.

"But it is his place to come and see *you*, surely? Are papa's affairs never to be cleared up? It seems to me you have done scarcely anything else these past months but fret over accounts and travel to town to see Heasley."

"There is a great deal to be seen

to, I assure you," he said in a weary voice. "Perhaps I shall not be here for the house-party," he added.

"But you must be! Who is to be host and take the gentlemen shooting? Besides, it will leave mama without any support whatever for what is bound to be an unhappy and difficult occasion for her."

"Meshaw will take charge of the shooting parties in his admirable way, as he always does — and I am persuaded no one will miss one indifferent shot. As to mama, she should have consulted me about the arrangements now that papa is no longer here," he said, an austere note coming into his voice. "*I* was not to know she was about to cast off her mourning and invite all and sundry to stay under my roof," he went on edgily.

"Perhaps it could be postponed," Susan suggested, anxious to avoid friction. "I'm sure mama would not mind the least in the world." That Edwin should be so touchy about his newly-inherited position as head of the family had never occurred to her.

"No, let it stand. I daresay she will

17

not commit the same error again. In any event, I *may* be able to return before the party disperses," he said, relenting a little. "My town visits are not all concerned with our man of business, and it hinges to some degree on whether a certain person is still fixed in town."

"How very mysterious! And is this certain person a prime article, I wonder?" she said in deliberately provocative tones, as she prepared to effect a hasty exit.

"Prime article, indeed, you saucy baggage! I hope you don't inflict such vulgar expressions upon anyone else?"

"Oh no! Only Aunt Selworthy," she disclosed innocently.

At least she had succeeded in making Edwin laugh: which was no mean feat, she reflected as she closed the door, even if she hadn't discovered a vast amount about his town visit — or concerning Lord John Deville for that matter.

# 2

WHEN Aurelia, Lady Gillow had told her sister-in-law, Agnes Selworthy, of the forthcoming house-party she had withheld the name of one family prominent on her list, and trailed Lord John Deville's invitation in part as a decoy for that critical lady's indignation. This she had done without compunction, for Lady Eleanora Tubb, a cousin of her late husband (and therefore also of Agnes), had been a dear friend and correspondent for almost twenty years, but had been disowned with shattering unanimity by her own entire family when she had eloped with an actor at the advanced age of eight-and-twenty. Her age (which precluded any hope of dismissing the affair as a youthful peccadillo), together with her husband's unfortunate profession, and even his name — Berkeley Tubb — which seemed for some reason to have offended them almost as much as his calling, had all

19

contributed to her disgrace and to her enduring position as the black sheep of the family.

But Aurelia, who had found her own introduction as a young bride to that same Gillow family a daunting experience, had been immediately attracted to the sweet-natured Lady Eleanora, and had met with not a trace of condescension from that quarter. They had formed a close and lasting relationship, but after only a year had been compelled to maintain their connexion by correspondence only.

However, since both ladies were dedicated letter-writers their knowledge of the other's affairs was comprehensive. Aurelia had shared her friend's every anxiety and apprehension over the birth of her son, Jermyn, now eighteen, as the event had been very close to the arrival of her own Susan; then a year later a daughter, Camilla, was born to Lady Eleanora. She had followed the development of the two children over the years as if they were her own, and had now reached the conclusion that Camilla was the perfect match for Edwin, her step-son, who had thus far evinced little interest in the subject of matrimony. If his father were still alive she would have had to stifle the idea at birth, of course, but now — well, everything was changed. Lady Eleanora and her young family were to be her guests at Reibridge Place for the first time; for her letter of acceptance had that day arrived. But Berkeley, who was now a shade more acceptable to the Polite World — if not to the Gillows — by virtue of his being an attorney, would not be accompanying his wife due to urgent business in town requiring his attention.

Which circumstance might make the party more acceptable to her sister-in-law, but Aurelia doubted it very much: no; during the coming days she would not give Agnes the pleasure of ceaseless jobations upon her dear friend's character, but would rather startle her with Lady Eleanora's presence. Aurelia did not consider Agnes would openly shun one of their guests, but if she was ill-advised enough to do so, so be it . . .

In fact Lady Gillow had been so engrossed in thwarting her sister-in-law's baser instincts that she had quite disregarded Edwin's vital part in her schemes. That she had been unwise to do so had already been borne in upon her. Her step-son, a compliant enough boy hitherto, seemed to have assumed a quite different nature of late. When first she broached the matter, his arrogant response to the very notion of a house-party had taken aback and hurt her. It was true, as he was swift to point out, that he was the head of the family now, but to assert his authority over such a trifling affair seemed churlish in the extreme.

In view of his attitude she had not thought it necessary to mention the Tubb family invitation to him in case they should refuse after all. However, their acceptance was to hand now, as were a gratifying number of others, and she felt this would surely influence him to fulfil his duties as host. She did not seek him out but waited until they were alone before she raised the vexed subject again.

Later that afternoon Aurelia was cosily established by the fireside in the drawing-room, with her worsted work on the frame before her: she was engaged in the replacement of all the bell-pulls in the house. Each one, of her own design, incorporated a different floral decoration, and as this was a light-coloured one of snowdrops she had been able to work by firelight in the thickening October gloom.

But it was no use, she would have to call for working-candles now . . . She leaned back in her chair, and, removing her spectacles, rubbed her eyes wearily. Then the door handle clicked and she sat up, trying to remember if she had rung for candles or not.

"Oh, it's you, Edwin."

"I hope I'm not disturbing you, ma'am." He might refer to her as mama to others, but ever since he had put his school days behind him he had called her ma'am to her face. "I have this minute returned from the wheelwrights and am in search of a fire to thaw out my frozen limbs!"

Aurelia gave him one of her unaffected but still bewitching smiles. "I'd be delighted to have your company for a while. As you can hear, the girls are having their music lesson, which means your aunt has put wool in her ears and retired to her room for the duration."

Sir Edwin stood by the fire, hands outspread to the heat, and looked with an appreciative eye upon his step-mother. He noticed she was wearing once again a favourite dress of bronze shot sarsenet, lavishly beflounced with vandyking of brown velvet about the hem: it suited her blonde colouring excessively. Her hair had been released from the severe confines of the widow's crimped cap and she appeared younger than ever.

"If I may say so, ma'am, you are in wonderful good looks today."

"Thank you, Edwin! Indeed you may, for I own I never felt more dreary in my life just before you came in — the very picture of middle-aged widowhood squinting through my glasses at the third bell-pull this month!" She set the offending work aside impatiently. "You mentioned visiting the wheelwrights? Is the chaise mended yet?"

"Yes; I've instructed Jack to make arrangements for its collection tomorrow."

"Splendid." Aurelia almost blurted out

that she would want it to send to meet Lady Eleanora off the mail at Reigate, but checked herself in time. Edwin might seem in mellow mood, but there was no cause to set up his bristles with an imprudent reference to the approaching house-party without some preamble.

"I shall be vastly relieved to be able to go abroad a little more than of late," she added by way of explanation.

"Talking of travelling abroad," Sir Edwin said quickly,"I have fixed to go up to town to see Heasley next week as I planned."

So, he was as implacable as ever on the topic of the house-party, Aurelia concluded, but she endeavoured once more to dissuade him. "Cannot Heasley wait for once? I swear you have lived in his pocket these past months. Sir Henry left the estate in good order, did he not? It was something he never discussed with me, of course, but he was known to be scrupulous in the ordering of his affairs. Certainly there have been no difficulties in the way of my very generous jointure."

"Yes, yes, everything is as it should

be," her step-son agreed shortly, all good humour put to flight now. "But you must see it is not easy to step into the shoes of such a man. I have a great deal to learn."

"I am persuaded you need entertain no qualms on the matter. Your father was well-pleased with you, you must know."

But this remark served only to darken the frowning countenance before her. So, as there seemed little to be lost now by adverting to the subject, she went on hastily: "Almost everyone has accepted for next week, I am delighted to say. Only two have declined. In fact only *one* positive refusal," she amended. "From the Mainwarings — poor Godfrey has his foot up in cotton again."

"I'm sorry to hear that," Sir Edwin said politely. "You will miss their cheerful presence and support, I daresay."

Was his conscience pricking him in just the smallest degree? Aurelia wondered.

"And who is the other guest still in the balance?" he asked, displaying a little more interest.

"Lord John Deville has not returned a reply yet, but then he may be from home at this time of the year."

"Indeed he may," he agreed, indifference apparently returning.

"I have ventured to invite the Tubbs to be of our number," Aurelia disclosed, hoping this prospect might at least intrigue her step-son sufficiently to alter his mind.

"Tubbs?" he echoed, blankly at first, then added: "Papa's disgraced cousin, you mean, who ran off with the actor fellow? You cannot be serious, ma'am. Why, it is an insult to his memory to ask that blackguard to cross the threshold of this house, let alone stay under his roof for weeks on end!"

Once again Aurelia was surprised by his vehement and unbending response: she doubted if even Sir Henry would have called Berkeley a blackguard now — eighteen years ago, perhaps, but Edwin was still in short coats then. Foolishly, she had not considered her step-son as one of the hostile Gillows, but she realised too late he was bound to reflect his father's views upon the subject.

"You overstate the matter a trifle, if I may say so," she pointed out as mildly as she was able, after hearing her friends vilified. "Berkeley Tubb was never other than a gentleman, and his wife is the sweetest creature you could wish to meet. How did the tale come to your ears, in any event?"

"Oh, I have known for ever," he said carelessly. "After all, it is the family skeleton, is it not? And I cannot regard this, of all occasions, to be a suitable moment for displaying our dirty dishes to the world."

"Edwin, you may be head of the family now, but I should not have to point out that that accident bestows no right upon you to abuse my acquaintance — and certainly not upon such slender grounds. Lady Eleanora's only crime was to marry where she wished, and not where her family pleased — although to my best belief she rejected no suitors of her family's choosing — there were none. And," she continued firmly, seeing Edwin take up a defensive mien and a deep breath, "Berkeley Tubb came from a family of excellent standing and is now a highly respected attorney. He became a player in his salad days, but once he assumed the responsibilities of a family he abandoned the theatre immediately for a more reliable profession. No, no power on this earth will make me desert Lady Eleanora! I am only sorry I have been unable to invite her to this house before, but of course I respected your father's wishes. I had not the least idea you would hold such violent opinions — or indeed, any opinions at all on such an ancient affair."

"No, well, perhaps I was guilty of parroting my elders' views upon the matter," Sir Edwin observed uneasily, just as soon as he was able to utter a word in his own vindication. "At any rate, if I am to be absent when Mr Tubb and Lady Eleanora are here it won't signify greatly. It has perhaps fallen out for the best."

Mollified in some degree, Aurelia told him: "Only Lady Eleanora and her two children are coming — Berkeley is prevented on this occasion."

"Children?"

"Oh yes, although they are not strictly children any longer, of course. Jermyn is of an age with Susan, and Camilla a year younger, both of them quite delightful by all accounts. I am impatient to make their acquaintance at long last. Indeed, I had hoped that you would be here to take Jermyn under your wing. It will be his first taste of country life and I am persuaded a little guidance would be invaluable from someone near in age."

"I am perfectly sure it would be," her step-son said, the dry note in his voice being quite unmistakable.

"Pray don't be unkind, Edwin — it ill-becomes you. Lady Eleanora is one of your more distinguished relations remember, and vastly better qualified than ever I was to prepare her children for the world."

"Come, ma'am, you do yourself an injustice. You may not have been an earl's daughter, or indeed a blue-stocking — for papa told me he would not have married you if you had been one of their number — but nor did he choose you for your beauty alone, you must know. He considered you a very intelligent woman of great sensibility."

Aurelia gave a little gasping laugh. "Well, you quite take my breath away!

But I was not dangling after compliments, I do assure you. However, I can see I must not underestimate you in the future — you appear to know more of the family secrets than I!"

"I cannot believe papa's misdoubt of learned literary females was ever a secret exactly!" Sir Edwin retorted, then he went on thoughtfully: "I must own my new-discovered second cousins — or is it cousins once removed? — intrigue me not a little."

"But not enough to keep you from the irresistible charms of Heasley, I collect?"

He shook his head. "I fear not, ma'am, but then I daresay there will be other opportunities in the future when I may make their acquaintance."

And with this sop Aurelia had to be content; her match-making endeavours, tentative though they were, had met with a check but not a rout. She had thought for a brief time Edwin might forbid the Tubbs the house altogether.

Before he took his leave Aurelia begged he would not mention Lady Eleanora's approaching visit to Aunt Selworthy. " — For if it should come to her ears,

I cannot imagine the uproar!"

"I can — vividly!" Sir Edwin chuckled. "You may trust me . . . I should dearly like to see her face when they are introduced."

On this united note, step-mother and son parted almost in perfect charity with one another, and both were relieved it should be so.

★ ★ ★

A mere thirty miles away, in the baroque Anlaby mansion in Piccadilly, a rather similar interview was taking place: but in this case both protagonists were older, and not surprisingly looked a great deal more like mother and son than did Aurelia and Sir Edwin.

The Duchess of Anlaby, a remarkably well-preserved if angular lady of approaching three score years and ten, viewed her second son with some scepticism.

"Not going into Gloucestershire? But you always start the hunting season with the Beauforts, John, just as your papa did in his more sprightly days. What will his

32

Grace think, to be slighted so?"

Captain Lord John Deville, contriving in spite of his impressive stature to look remarkably at ease amidst the walnut convolutions of an elegant eighteenth century settee, favoured his mama with a lazy smile; and this was no ordinary smile, but a variation of the famous Deville Dazzle (as it was dubbed somewhat sardonically by his friends) which had been known to cause a flutter in even the most imperturbable female bosom. The reason for this universal susceptibility was not far to seek; for Lord John's devastating expression did not conceal, as so often, a callous libertine tendency but a wholly open and chivalrous nature, which could disarm the most flinty-hearted spinster.

"You flatter me, mama! But I beg leave to doubt that the Duke will even remark my absence amidst the tumult at Badminton House which prevails at this time. Papa is something quite other, and his prowess in the field will always be missed. For my part I have, of course, sent my apologies and a promise to honour them with a visit later in the season," he concluded with a hint of mockery.

"*If* the weather should allow of much travelling abroad this winter." Her Grace shivered and drew the angola shawl about her shoulders. "This early frost bodes ill — it would not surprise me if we were to have another winter like '14."

"Indeed I hope not!" remarked Lord John with some feeling, as he rose to stir into life the coals in the capacious grate. "I have not yet recovered from being snow-bound in Leicestershire for two months, with some of the most bottle-headed and tedious company it has ever been my misfortune to encounter!"

"That's better," the Duchess said appreciatively, "but you really should ring for someone to do that — yes, look, you have some soot on your sleeve."

As he blew at the offending mark and then dusted the sage-green kerseymere with a lawn kerchief, his mother went on: "I am glad you are not leaving town, John. With William gone it will be rather lonely here in this great house."

He stopped what he was doing and

looked quickly at his parent. "I'm sorry, mama, but I *am* going into the country, only not to the Beauforts."

Disappointment wreathed her features. "Oh, I see."

Lord John knew it was not the smallest use putting forward his father as an invigorating companion: for years the old Duke had either kept his room or haunted the whist tables at White's. "Pluck up! William may be gone, as you put it, but he is only a stone's throw away."

"And if he has any wits, which I doubt, he will be fully occupied dancing attendance upon that lovely bride of his — after waiting thirty-seven years to shake off my apron strings," she observed, her spirit returning. "Mark you, if *I* lived in a noisy, dreary place like Jermyn Street, I should be a-visiting all day. But there, it is precisely the sort of deadly dull house I would have expected William to choose, having declined half of this one."

"You are very hard on him, ma'am. He has obliged you by marrying at last, and Emmeline, by your own admission, has

35

every quality you could wish in a future duchess."

"Ay," she agreed readily enough. "And she's a good broad-hipped gal who will breed well and encounter little difficulty at her lying-in, I'll wager."

As he disposed himself comfortably upon the settee again Lord John cast a startled glance at his parent.

"Her ladyship is in the family way already?" It was not that he felt in the least jaundiced that his brother should be producing an heir, but William's sudden plunge into matrimony in the summer had taken them all by surprise: to imagine him a father was quite beyond his powers at the moment.

"No, she ain't," her Grace said aggrievedly, "but I shall be the first to know, she promised me that. I only hope — " She broke off. "Where are you going that takes precedence over the Beauforts?" The dark brown eyes, an inheritance from her French mother and a feature she had in turn passed on to Lord John, fixed upon him alertly now.

Well-used to his mother's tenacious if erratic mode of conversation, he had been awaiting this particular question: he ran a slim brown finger over the carved arm of the settee and thought he would quiz her just a little.

"Oh, it could not be said to take *precedence*, exactly. Indeed, what could, over Badminton House?" he mused in a maddening drawl. " . . . But it offers novelty, a complete change of scene and a beautiful woman — and what more could a palate, jaded by the ennui of a season in the Metropolis, ask?"

"Cease prating like a cook," she advised with some degree of brusquerie, "and come to the point. Where are you going?"

"Into Surrey," he supplied promptly, if not very informatively. Then, with perfect timing, before his parent could erupt again, he added: "Reibridge," and sat back and waited.

"Reibridge?" the Duchess repeated, evidently accepting the challenge. Frowning deeply she stared into the flames for a moment.

"Not the Fenwicks?" she asked, then answered herself. "No, no, that was Redbridge." She shook her head impatiently.

"My memory is not what it was. I do *know* these people, do I?" she demanded with sudden suspicion.

"Well, I fancy you must know of them at least. The lady was a famous beauty — still is, I collect."

The Duchess cackled to herself. "Just like charades, ain't it? A well-known beauty? Thought they must all be dead by now — the Devonshire House coterie at any rate were my age and more." She started to enumerate them on the fingers of a mittened hand: "Maria Gunning, married the Earl of Coventry — she died young; then there was the Duchess of Argyll, another of the astonishingly handsome Gunning sisters, but too tall to be genteel, in my view. Mrs Bouverie," she went on, "Frances Crewe — now she *is* alive and, I hear, still remarkably beautiful . . . but lives in Hampstead to the best of my recollection."

"No, I am not proposing to stay with Mrs Crewe, delightful old lady though she may be," Lord John said, taking pity on her. "Perhaps it will help if I tell you she is more of my generation than yours."

"Might as well be in the days of Queen Dick!" her Grace snorted. "For I have never seen one young 'un who is better than a candle to the sun. Well, maybe there was *one* gal in recent years who had some slight claim to the title of Beauty," she admitted. "Miss Lydeard was well-bred though not of the first rank, but could have married where she wished with her face and fortune. She chose Sir Henry Gillow for some reason which confounded her more illustrious admirers. Gillow! . . . Reibridge!" Her brown eyes glittered in triumph.

Her son made great play of applauding her success but at once her grace cried: "No, you cannot be intending to cut up Sir Henry's peace! A flirtation in town is one thing but to invade a man's home for the purpose of — "

Lord John interrupted this frank and embarrassing lecture without delay. "Mama, Sir Henry died at the beginning of the year."

"Oh, did he? I hadn't heard." This news allayed her fears for a brief space, then she returned to the attack with renewed vigour. "But a widow — that makes it worse, John, foolish beyond permission!"

He sought to defend himself but looked amused nonetheless. "You must think my behaviour quite deplorable, ma'am — flirting with married ladies in the spring, seducing country widows in the winter months!"

"And so it is, compared to gentlemen of my day," she declared roundly.

"Ay, a claim every female since Eve has made, I daresay! Be fair, flirtation and seduction were not innovations of this century."

"It is high time you married," the Duchess said severely, trying to regain some control of the conversation and her son. "This penchant you have for older females will be your undoing."

"Or theirs," his lordship could not resist murmuring, but in more audible tones he protested: "That was a charge which could have been levelled against me fifteen years past, perhaps, but now I fear I have caught up with the older females — as you so inelegantly term them — we are of an age! As for matrimony, I have no rooted objection

40

to the state, but the Devilles are late marriers, you well know: papa did not wed till he was nigh on forty — and look at William."

"He at least has chosen a youthful wife," her Grace protested.

"Sensible fellow — he has the line to secure," Lord John observed smoothly. "Which leaves me free to follow, or even marry my fancy, does it not?"

"But not to make a cake of yourself with a widow even if she was a Beauty," her Grace cautioned him drily. "How came you to have a card from her in the first place? I had no notion you were acquainted."

"Nor are we, yet. But what is more natural than that Society's most beautiful widow should look first to its most handsome bachelor?" he demanded in mock earnestness.

She laughed. "Very well! Keep your secrets from your poor old mother. I daresay it is none of my business. But just a word of warning, John," she went on, serious now. "It was well known the Lydeard Beauty turned down a duke before she wed Sir Henry. Perhaps she regretted it since, who knows, and is seeking to remedy the matter the second time."

"Oh, I am persuaded you cannot be right in saying that, ma'am," he answered, matching the gravity of her tone but with a discernible glint in his eye, "for I am no duke nor likely to be one now — although the lady may not have heard of William's marriage, of course." He paused a moment, displaying every sign of profound thought. "But no," he said at length, "it *must* be my legendary looks, don't you think? There can be no other explanation."

He caught the cushion hurled at him by his exasperated parent, and grinned.

# 3

"WHEN you have finished breakfast I wish you to put on your warmest pelisse, and go in the chaise to Reigate to meet the Stage bearing our first guests, if you will," Aurelia said casually to her daughter Susan one morning.

"Of course, Mama, but I thought our visitors were due to arrive tomorrow?"

"Yes, most of them are, but this is a particular friend and I want to have the opportunity of a quiet cose with her before the rest of the company arrive."

Susan who, like Aunt Selworthy, regarded Lord John Deville's anticipated arrival as the high point of the next few days, was not greatly interested in her mama's acquaintance, but was glad for a drive into Reigate whatever the purpose.

"Aunt Selworthy will be accompanying me, I collect," she said, without enthusiasm.

"No!" Aurelia exclaimed, causing Susan

to look up from buttering her toast. "There will scarcely be room in the chaise," she continued at once in more moderate tones. "Lady Eleanora is bringing her two children with her."

Susan supposed they would be companions for her young sisters, Mary and Henrietta, in the schoolroom: (her brothers, James and Paul, were away at Eton). She was pleased, though, that Aunt Selworthy would not be there to cast the customary gloom over everyone right from the start.

"I know you will do all in your power to make our friends welcome," Aurelia was saying, "but I am especially anxious you should be nice to Camilla — she is just a year younger than you and a trifle shy if her mother is to be believed."

"Oh, capital! I had thought they might be no more than nursery children," Susan smiled, delighted at the prospect of a companion of her own at last.

"No, Jermyn is your age, and I must own I am quite out of conceit with Edwin for deserting us at this time: he could have acted Mentor to him during his stay with us. But, there it is — he was determined to turn his back even on his old friends so I could scarcely expect him to change his plans for new ones, could I?" Aurelia said, with a determined brightness she had been at pains to adopt over the whole affair.

"Have they no papa?" Susan asked tentatively, avoiding the vexed matter of Edwin's absence.

"Yes, but Mr Tubb is unable to accompany them," her mother replied in constrained accents. She hesitated and then added hurriedly: "Lady Eleanora is your papa's cousin, my dear, but he rather lost sight of her over the years. I thought it would be pleasant to renew her acquaintance," she concluded lamely.

But Susan was so cheered by the sudden appearance of some completely unknown relatives that she paid no heed to her parent's slight evasiveness about them.

"You had best go and change right away," Aurelia advised. "I have asked for the horses to be put to at half past ten."

Less than an hour later, Susan felt quite important conferring with the landlord of the Swan at Reigate, and having him set aside a little parlour for the use of the travellers when they arrived. She inspected the apartment and even had the temerity to ask that a fire be made up. Had the landlord not assured her that the True Blue was due within the half hour, "and always arrives as prompt as a dog for his dinner," Susan might have been tempted into a solitary perambulation around Reigate, so heady was this her first independent jaunt; with no querulous aunt at her elbow, or young sisters to absorb all her energies, she felt it incumbent upon her to exploit her brief freedom to the full. But in the event she paced about the low-ceilinged parlour, occasionally stopping by the window which overlooked the main street.

However, there was little doubt when the True Blue was approaching: as the coach rumbled near it made a noise fit to shatter the Swan's foundations. When it passed by, the passengers perched high on the roof were almost level with Susan as she watched from the first floor window.

The whole of this expedition was so

novel to her that she had scarcely given a thought to the strangers, who travelled by stage and not post chaise as one would expect, and who would be shown in to her at any moment; but had she thought of nothing else, it would not have prepared her for the Tubb family.

The landlord himself announced them, with a quiet reverence inspired in him only by a combination of unmistakable Quality, excellent address and superior looks; and the newly-arrived trio pleased him upon all counts.

As Susan listened to Lady Eleanora's greetings, she had a fleeting impression of her ladyship's exquisite blue velvet pelisse with three shoulder-capes trimmed with swansdown; of the daughter's more prosaic dress of pale green merino, but which Susan barely noticed as the face shyly peeping out from the depths of the frilled poke was quite the prettiest she had ever seen; and, finally, of the son's equally attractive countenance as he smiled and murmured a few words upon being introduced.

Lady Eleanora beamed upon Susan in a manner which was quite unaccountable to that young lady; and then wholly confounded her when the smiles turned to tears, and her ladyship rummaged about in a huge fashionable muff for a handkerchief.

To Susan's great relief the waiter appeared at that moment with the coffee which she had asked for.

Recovering her poise with commendable speed, Lady Eleanora said: "Good gracious, my dear, you are spoiling us! Tell me, are you quite on your own here?" she asked, when the waiter had departed.

"Oh yes," replied Susan airily, as if it were the most commonplace thing in the world. "You see there are only four places in the chaise," she said, repeating her mother's explanation mechanically.

"Lucky you," cut in Camilla, her hazel eyes round with admiration. "I am not allowed to stir an *inch* without a maid in attendance."

"But you do live in town, my love," her mother pointed out, hoping that Aurelia did not allow Susan too many awkward liberties of this sort.

With a little timely help from Jermyn in

distributing the cups, Susan presided over the coffee pot with as much assurance as she could muster to preserve her new reputation for worldliness. This proved difficult, though, for as she watched Jermyn she realised that here was the hero of her novel: not that she had actually reached the hero, of course — and never would with the speechless boneheaded Lord Quantock blocking her way. But if she had, she knew he would have looked exactly like Jermyn: middling height, slender build, blue eyes, light brown hair curling crisply about his face — perhaps a little longer than she would have imagined — and a nose and mouth which were, well, just right . . .

His mode of dress impressed her, and she would have been quite unable to picture this. Used only to Edwin's expensive but comparatively sober taste, her attention was riveted upon Jermyn's gaily striped waistcoat, his full-skirted frock coat — instead of the customary cut-back tail coat — over buckskin breeches and hunting boots with startlingly white tops: the latter items being the gentleman's concession to country life apparently.

The talk was all of the journey: Susan had never travelled Stage — and nor, it seemed, had the Tubbs hitherto — so it proved an easy subject for discussion until they came to know each other better. But when the time approached for them to leave, Susan's precarious poise began to falter a little; she knew she should tip the various people at the inn — but whom and how much?

She decided to resolve it by throwing herself upon Jermyn's mercy.

"Do you suppose you could attend to the tipping for me, sir?" she appealed to him. "I am persuaded it would look so much better if you were to do it."

Young Mr Tubb was delighted to oblige: indeed he had scarcely taken his eyes off their young hostess since they arrived, and would clearly have faced worse hazards than tipping for her sake.

Susan thanked him wholeheartedly and, free of that burden, turned her undivided attention to shepherding her guests to the chaise and thence to Reibridge Place.

The first person they encountered on arrival was Aunt Selworthy, and this was not as accidental as it seemed. She had discovered that Susan had gone off alone in the chaise and was agog to know why. As soon as she heard the returning wheels on the gravel she bided her time in the hall.

Emerging as the travellers were being received by the powdered and liveried footman — who had been well aware of the lady's hovering presence — Mrs Selworthy bustled forward, saying:

"Susan, my dear, I was so vexed when I realized you were abroad alone! You know I would have accompanied you, for I never pay the least regard to my dislike of closed carriages." Then, as if the party of strangers had instantly been conjured out of the air, she cried: "Oh, there now, you were meeting guests!"

Susan introduced them with blithe confidence; but when the fateful name of Tubb was mentioned Aunt Selworthy started, clapped a hand to her forehead almost dislodging the all-embracing crimped cap she always wore, and said: *Lady Eleonora,* in a mien of high tragedy. "You must excuse me," she went on shakenly, "I have the megrim ... Indeed, was on my way to my room to lie down with my vinaigrette when I was interrupted," she concluded in offensive tones.

Susan smiled in embarrassment at Lady Eleanora, thinking that it was merely Aunt Selworthy at her worst, but the footman who, in the way of servants, knew all about the family's black sheep, permitted himself a supercilious look at her ladyship. Ever watchful for such slights, even after twenty years, Lady Eleanora wished fervently she had not come.

But a few minutes later, re-united with Aurelia, her misgivings were soon forgotten. Mrs Selworthy, apparently laid low with a particularly severe headache, did not appear at dinner and so, with Susan looking after Camilla and Jermyn, Aurelia had her quiet cose with her old friend.

Susan's first call with her two guests was to the schoolroom to introduce Mary and Henrietta to them. Camilla and Jermyn, by reason of their having no young brothers and sisters of their own, were charmed with the two young girls, and accepted Mary's challenge to a game of spillikins there and then, with alacrity; something which Susan, out of sheer monotony, had been unable to do these six months past when Mary first discovered she had a talent for the game.

Mary, a skinny miss at the unlovely age of eleven, was the elder of the two girls: her other obsession at the time, besides spillikins, was how she could best banish her freckles. Every remedy was tried with furious intensity for at least two days, for she was quite convinced that they presented her only barrier to growing up a Beauty like her mama.

Henrietta, on the other hand, at seven years of age, seemed set fair to be the Gillow Beauty a decade hence. But in dress they were alike: high-waisted white muslin dresses with scarlet sashes and red morocco shoes.

To Mary's delight she beat Jermyn to flinders at spillikins — a particular satisfaction because on the rare occasions Edwin had condescended to play with her she had lost, so it was her first triumph over the opposite sex.

Next morning Susan looked in upon the schoolroom again.

"Where're our new cousins?" were Henrietta's first words, but Mary, more selective, asked: "Where is cousin Jermyn?"

"They are having a late breakfast with mama," Susan told them, spinning one of the globes. "You may not see much of them today as all our other guests arrive, but be patient, I am sure you will have more games in due course."

"You mustn't do that," Henrietta said, frowning disapprovingly at her eldest sister, meaning the whirling globe. "Miss May says so."

Susan halted it with the palm of her hand. "You're quite right, Hetty," she agreed, recalling her own recent schooldays, and Miss May, with a shudder.

"Are you going to marry him, Suke?" Mary enquired with great solemnity.

"Who?" cried Susan, spinning round, almost as fast as the globe, to face her gawky sister.

"Cousin Jermyn, of course. Well,

mama must've invited them for some purpose, mustn't she? We've never seen them before, have we? I expect it is all fixed but they haven't bothered to tell you. Parents do that sort of thing sometimes." She hesitated, but only for a moment. "I thought I would ask, because if you don't want to marry him, I thought I might. He would only have to wait a few years," she went on, sensing objections to this very reasonable proposal. "By then my freckles will have gone. Besides, I beat him at spillikins, and I wouldn't want to marry anyone I couldn't beat," she said, as if to conclude the matter.

Susan had had time to recover a little during this outpouring, and she smiled at her earnest junior.

"Perhaps you should wait awhile before you make any definite resolve — cousin Jermyn was out of practice, you know. In a week's time you may not be able to take a single game from him."

"I shall!"

Miss May returned at that moment — a very timely entrance from Susan's point of view: a few seconds earlier the governess would have heard Mary's outburst about Jermyn; a minute later and Susan would probably have had to answer Mary's home question as to why the Tubbs had been invited out of the blue.

She left the schoolroom a good deal perturbed: in her prattling way Mary could be right. Indeed, the more she considered it, the more likely it seemed. Jermyn and she were of an age, and last night she had discovered that their respective mothers had been in close correspondence for years past. She also remembered how disproportionately emotional Lady Eleanora had been at the Swan when they had met: decidedly excessive for an encounter, however belated, with your cousin's child — but for a future daughter-in-law?

Still, if this scheme had been hatched years ago, why had they never met? Susan recalled, then, something her mother had said — about papa losing touch with them. That must be it, she supposed: papa had disapproved the match but now nothing stood in its path.

She stopped dead, overcome momentarily by the awesome implications for

56

her future which had been revealed by Mary's childish remark.

"Penny for them, ma'am!" said Jermyn as he came out of the breakfast parlour a step behind his sister, Camilla.

"Oh! Nothing at all! I was merely wondering if you would both care to take a turn about the park this morning?" she improvised desperately.

"Yes, indeed, that would be delightful," Jermyn acknowledged in dubious tones, and looking somewhat startled. " . . . If it ceases to rain stair-rods."

Camilla blushed for everyone, and Susan said too loudly: "Yes, later, of course, was what I meant to say." She managed a reassuring smile, and suggested that in the meantime they should repair to the library.

"Two fires will be kindled in there today, for I expect mama will use the library to receive the other guests as they arrive," she explained, regaining a semblance of command over the situation.

It soon became apparent to Susan that Jermyn was not of a bookish turn: Camilla shared her own passion for novel reading, it seemed, but Jermyn was simply attentive from politeness, bearing the library steps hither and thither, and climbing up them as nimbly as his tight buckskin breeches would allow.

"It is not the smallest use showing Jermyn these," Camilla confided, when Susan produced a pile of old fashioned romances, "for he calls me bird-witted if I so much as open one at home."

Her brother glowered at her whilst denying to his hostess ever having expressed such an opinion.

Camilla giggled and put a dainty hand to her mouth. "Do look at this one! *The Innocent Adultery*! Well, how dreadful!"

"Now *that* is hen-witted!" Jermyn was moved to protest in spite of himself. "Can't be both, can it? Stands to reason!"

Unmoved by these fraternal criticisms, Camilla went on: "May I borrow it whilst I am here, Susan?"

"Yes, but perhaps it would be wise to keep it from your mama's gaze."

"Oh, I will. You won't be beastly and tell her, will you, Jermyn?" she said in wheedling tones.

"No, of course not," he maintained stoutly, although Susan had a suspicion this was said more to impress her with his upright behaviour than from any natural brotherly devotion.

"How came you to have such a splendid collection?" Camilla asked, her customary reticence quite banished by the sight of the few battered two-shilling volumes: she devoured the titles, goggle-eyed — *The Fatal Compliance, The Unguarded Moment* . . .

"I am not at all certain," Susan confessed. "They are assuredly not mama's for I don't believe she read a book in her life — and I can't imagine they are Aunt Selworthy's, who declares novels to be the work of the devil. Perhaps they were grandmama's — I vow they are old enough! However," she said, smiling at Camilla, "I believe you may find them a trifle disappointing — their titles are a sad tease." She was about to say that her dearest wish was to lay hands on a copy of *Glenarvon* — a more recent novel, and truly shocking if the review she had read was to be believed; but she refrained, inhibited by Jermyn's obvious disinterest in novels of any complexion.

"When the rest of the company arrive you will be able to go out shooting, Jermyn, or hunting if that is more to your taste. I daresay it will clear tomorrow," Susan remarked pleasantly in encouraging accents, as he gazed out at the peak through rain-streaked windows.

"I fear I'm something of a tyro at country pursuits . . . And I have brought no hunter with me," he said apologetically, and clearly out of his depth.

"There is not the least call to fret on that head," Susan reassured him. "We can mount you well enough — you may ride a little lighter than Edwin but I fancy one of his horses will suit. I am only sorry Edwin is not here, but Major Welton is an old friend of his and will be everything that is helpful."

Her guest still looked apprehensive, so she added: "There will be no Melton Men or Nonesuchs of the company to put anyone to the blush, you may be sure of that." She was confidently employing the few words of slang she had gleaned from

Edwin, thereby strengthening unwittingly her worldly image in her cousin's eyes.

Jermyn brightened a little upon hearing this news, and seemed more at ease for the rest of the day.

This happy state of affairs was preserved until the whole party, which numbered about fifteen with the new arrivals, were gathered in the drawing-room prior to walking in to dinner.

Jermyn had at last discarded his white-topped boots and unusual frock-coat for more conformable dress clothes, but Susan could not stifle the reflection that his neckcloth was a trifle ambitious: Edwin had never attempted anything so hazardous-looking. She feared for the safety of his ears as his shirt points stuck out like daggers.

However, the best that could be said for the ensemble was that it prevented Jermyn Tubb's jaw from falling open in too drastic a fashion when Lord John Deville was announced; pausing for a moment, framed by the lofty arched doorway, until his hostess, Lady Gillow, stepped forward to welcome him.

If this wasn't a Nonesuch, Melton Man

and Corinthian rolled into one, reflected the chagrined Jermyn, then he would eat his new blue-spotted Tobine waistcoat — which in any event he would never dare wear now.

# 4

LORD JOHN, who had been unavoidably delayed in his journey to Reibridge by a lame leader, insisted upon being shown in to his hostess to tender his apologies at the first possible moment. Consequently, Speed, the butler, announced him somewhat breathlessly and an attendant footman was seen to disappear into the distance bearing away a voluminous drab coat and tall beaver hat. His lordship stood revealed in a gold-buttoned blue tailcoat, pantaloons of the palest grey and glistening Hessian boots (and how he had kept them free from mud on such a treacherous day, Jermyn would very much like to have known).

When Aurelia approached her tardy guest, herself resplendent in a low-cut, long-sleeved dress of cornflower silk with two deep scalloped lace flounces about the hem, it seemed that a hush fell upon those assembled about them. Few

63

of those present had ever seen a more striking couple, and all eyes were turned their way: some covertly — like Aunt Selworthy's; others frankly admiring like the young Tubb's.

But Susan fell into neither of these categories: her gage certainly was upon the stranger but her immediate response was to feel sorry for Jermyn in face of this Nonpareil (more particularly as she had rashly promised him no such creature would be present). However, when she saw the smile bestowed upon her mama by his lordship, before he bowed low and raised her hand to his lips — a gesture old-fashioned enough to startle her — she recalled the conversation she had had with Edwin about Lord John. A rich eligible bachelor, averse to young ladies, he had designated him; and she could see for herself that he was remarkably handsome and possessed of considerable address. No one could deny he would be an admirable match for her mama, and judging by the earnest way the pair were still conversing they had a great deal to say to one another. They had the look of old friends, and indeed might be such for all that Susan knew.

A polite murmur of conversation resumed about the room but the interest in the new arrival remained, albeit subdued.

At the time Susan was with Major Welton, a bluff round-faced sportsman about fortyish, who had little drawing-room small talk, and Mr and Mrs George Davenport, a decade younger, but no easier for Susan to engage in lively conversation. So she was obliged to devote her whole attention to these guests, and the next time she looked around to the entrance doors Lord John had vanished and her mama had again joined Lady Eleanora by the fire.

It was about the hour for dinner to be served, and she wondered if they were all to be kept from the table until his lordship should reappear sublime in dress clothes. If her brother were to be believed that operation could take a fashionable gentleman anything up to two hours to achieve. Susan had the healthy appetite of youth, and was not favourably inclined towards Lord John at that moment.

In the event his lordship put the

company to no inconvenience whatsoever. He re-entered the drawing-room quietly only minutes later, and dinner was announced almost at once. Only a few of the assembled party had been made known to him — and Susan was not of their number — when he gave Aurelia his arm and the pair walked down to the dining-room leading the guests.

Jermyn made sure he escorted Susan, and Camilla was partnered by a picqued Timothy Etheridge: it was the first competition the squire's son had faced for Susan's attention and he did not care for it. As he lived close by in the village, he was not a house-guest, either, merely riding over to join in the various activities when he wished; which placed him, he considered, at a distinct disadvantage vis-à-vis all the eligible gentlemen who, as far as he could see, seemed to be swarming all over the place.

It was a gathering of the utmost informality, and as neither of the young girls was out yet they sat together for support, and Mr Etheridge's nose was further put out of joint by having to sit by Camilla throughout dinner

— Jermyn having secured the only free place by Susan. Timothy, a solemn young man, reflected he was going to have to watch that Town Tulip: he eyed Jermyn's already wilting shirt points with distaste.

Mr Etheridge did not lack opportunity for further brooding thoughts as the meal progressed, for Camilla was as tongue-tied as he was with strangers, and she chattered to Susan a vast amount of the time.

Lord John was placed at Aurelia's right-hand, and a distinctly miffy-looking wealthy widower of long standing, Sir Anthony Burns — who had his eye upon his hostess now his old friend Sir Henry was no more — was seated to her left.

Susan, glancing up the table occasionally at her parent — clearly wallowing in these masculine attentions — experienced a sinking of the spirit: Aunt Selworthy's crabbed hints about her sister-in-law dangling after a husband seemed only too possible.

"Isn't he divine?" breathed Camilla in her cousin's ear, following her gaze to Lord John.

"He's well enough," Susan answered, with what seemed like wonderful indifference to her audience, "but I do think he should have changed for dinner."

"Well, yes," Camilla admitted reluctantly, "but you said yourself how it would have delayed everything. Besides, he still contrives somehow to look like the only properly dressed gentleman here. The way the candlelight glints off those buttons of his! Do you suppose they are *real gold*?" She asked in awed tones.

Susan snorted. "I really couldn't say, but he need not puff off his consequence here! Mama won't like it one jot," she declared, convinced by this time of the complete opposite: her mama seemed to be regrettably in thraldom to him already — laughing excessively, and almost ignoring poor Sir Anthony.

This brisk retort had the effect of silencing if not converting Camilla, who now gave her attention to a rare remark from the taciturn Mr Etheridge.

Jermyn claimed Susan's notice with a further observation not calculated to reassure her. "Deville is losing no time in setting the female hearts aflutter, I see! Dashed if I know how he does it," he said, with barely disguised envy. "But they do make a prodigious fine-looking couple, do they not?" He had quite forgotten that his hostess was barely out of mourning for a husband, but saw at once that the remark was not met exactly with raptures by his listener, so he blundered on: "Lady Gillow, well, she is still in astonishing beauty." This, too, seemed not quite the best thing to say to her daughter, and he concluded somewhat desperately: "I think you're much prettier, of course."

Susan could not maintain her disapproval in face of such a well-meant if inept compliment, and she thanked him. "But I don't mind the least in the world having a Beauty for a mother," she lied, in an airy fashion.

"No reason why you should," Jermyn said staunchly trying to make up for his earlier lapse, and giving her an appraising look which brought a blush to her cheek.

They exchanged shy smiles and then he asked: "Did you really not know Lord John Deville was coming?"

"He was just a name to me, I fear. I have never set eyes upon him before."

"Even so, didn't his name mean *anything*?" her cousin asked incredulously. "Well, no, I suppose it wouldn't to a girl. But he's a real bang up to the mark top-sawyer. Hasn't got an equal in a mill, or in driving a four-in-hand." Jermyn's eyes were shining, but then he added dispiritedly, "I shan't dare put my nose outside the door — or even play billiards!"

"Nonsense!" Susan reproved him, dismayed by this lack of bottom. "Why shouldn't you be better than he is eventually? — you're younger, that's all. Don't be afraid to ask him anything you want to know, it's a wonderful opportunity, after all."

Jermyn looked aghast. "I? Ask Deville? Why, I daresay he'll never even speak to me!"

"I'll want to know the reason why if he does not," retorted Susan with commendable spirit. "He need not play off his *condescending airs* in this house."

It was then that the appalling thought crossed her mind that she was referring

70

to someone who might be her future step-father. Seeing a completely strange man kissing her mother's hand had left her own emotions in shaken order. She wished Edwin were here, although what he could do about anything she was not at all sure.

When the ladies retired and left the gentlemen, Susan knew a great deal more about Lord John's sporting prowess from Jermyn, who seemed unwilling to talk about anything else, but had learned nothing to reassure her — except perhaps that he did appear to be a confirmed bachelor.

In the drawing-room she turned to Aunt Selworthy as an ally for once.

"Well, aunt, what say you to Lord John and his ways?" she enquired, confidently anticipating a diatribe upon his iniquities.

But a rare smile passed over Mrs Selworthy's plump features rendering her surprisingly cherubic. "He is delightful, is he not? So very proper in his address — why, it must be years since I saw a gentleman kiss a lady's hand like that."

Susan, dazed by so much approval in one speech, wondered for a moment if he had kissed *her* hand but could not believe that. "Have you spoken with him, then?"

"Oh yes." Mrs Selworthy positively preened herself. "I was the first to meet him — Aurelia insisted. He moves so well, you must have noticed," she said dreamily, in a manner more like Camilla's, thought Susan crossly. "It has something to do with carrying a sword."

"Carrying a *sword*?" echoed Susan, baffled. "He isn't, is he?"

"No, no, gentlemen don't these days in the ordinary way, but that is precisely what I am saying — the older ones who were used to do so have such poise and elegance in their movements. Of course Lord John was used to be an officer — captain, I fancy. How I should like to have seen him in his regimentals." She sighed.

"How come you to know so much about him?" her niece asked, feeling quite old and responsible faced with these bizarre girlish sentiments.

"Ah well, it was through a distinguished connexion of my late husband . . . "

The requisite cloud descended upon her aunt's brow at mention of her departed spouse, and whilst she enumerated what seemed to Susan like the entire genealogy of his family.

" . . . so you see I have always taken a particular interest in the duchess and the Devilles. Only recently I recall seeing his elder brother's marriage announced in the Gazette — that's Lord Grantham, who must be fortyish now and a much *steadier* gentleman than his brother. Although he did wed a young girl, which I can't quite like, but he is thinking of securing the line, I daresay," she added, with grudging magnanimity. "However I fancy the duchess will still entertain grave misgivings."

"But why, if Lord Grantham is married now?"

"Ah yes, but so many things can go wrong — they might only have girl children — or no children at all, like Mr Selworthy and I."

For once Susan felt sympathy for her aunt when the customary gloom enveloped her: her childlessness she knew was a genuine sorrow.

"Are there no other brothers of Lord John?" she said to distract her.

Mrs Selworthy shook her head. "And the old duke is not much more than a valetudinarian these days, I collect. He may not be long for this world."

Susan was almost relieved to hear these doleful sentiments: a giddy Aunt Selworthy was not to be thought of.

Her mama came across to them and bade Susan to stop gossiping and look to the other ladies.

"And when the gentlemen return by the by, I particularly wish you to meet Lord John — I vow he is the most charming man I have ever met! I shouldn't say it, of course, but he has made me feel quite young again!"

There was no need to say it, thought Susan, noticing the new light in her mother's beautiful eyes and the heightened complexion. She found herself in the ridiculous position of wanting to warn her own mother against the attractions of a man who, if he had exploded Aunt Selworthy's antipathy and suspicion in a matter of seconds, could clearly charm the birds from the boughs.

When the tea tray was brought in and the gentlemen were probably not far behind, every female gaze drifted towards the doors periodically — from the naive Camilla to the oldest matron there, George Davenport's mother.

Susan was disgusted: she hoped *she* knew how to conduct herself with more propriety even if she wasn't properly out. Turning her back pointedly to the doors she talked with Lady Eleanora and Camilla: unfortunately her social skill was not yet sufficient to direct the conversation into other channels.

"I think I shall be forever indebted to Aurelia for inviting Lord John. For if anyone can depress Jermyn's more extreme notions of dress, his lordship can, being such a respected member of the haut ton," Lady Eleanora was saying.

Susan wanted to fly to Jermyn's defence but did not quite like to give the appearance of contradicting her ladyship.

Camilla, emboldened to voice her own criticisms of her brother's fashionable vagaries, met with a set-down from her mama, which gave Susan some small satisfaction. That Lady Eleanora herself dressed in the first style of elegance, she had to admit; and had she not been set against Aurelia, who effortlessly eclipsed any member of her sex, she would have stood out in a gathering. However, she did look like the mother of a grown family, which no one could say of Lady Gillow. Even in her daughter's eyes Aurelia seemed youthful — particularly this evening. With most of the guests engaged to stay at least two or three weeks at Reibridge Place, Susan hoped fervently her mama was not going to set them all in a bustle with her conduct towards Lord John. She could almost sense the tabbies waiting to pounce: certainly there would be no lack of jealousy, judging by the intense ripple of interest which told Susan that his lordship had that moment returned amongst them.

Having not the least desire to offer their prime guest an affront, Susan turned a little so that should her mama wish to catch her eye she could do so with ease.

Predictably Lord John went at once

to Aurelia's side and she, in turn, gave a speaking look in her daughter's direction. Obeying the summons with as much dignity as her eighteen years would allow, Susan walked towards her parent. Not of a markedly shy disposition she nonetheless had a great instinct to approach the formidably attractive pair with downcast gaze. In simple white silk, and with pearls her only adornment, she had rarely felt so outshone by her mother's beauty; added to which his lordship was lazily raising his quizzing glass — which she had only then noticed and which hung on a long black silk riband round his neck — prior to surveying her through it. None of this was calculated to bolster her confidence, and finally she remembered his disdain of young ladies in general. This last served to render Susan defiant and she walked on up to them, head held high, returning as well as she was able what she regarded as his lordship's insufferable scrutiny. She stood, if anything, a little taller than her mother and for once was grateful for it.

"Delighted to make your acquaintance, ma'am," Lord John said, letting the glass fall at last. "I have heard so much about you these past years."

Years! thought Susan — so surprised she scarcely noticed she was being favoured with the famous Deville Dazzle — her mama had known him for *years*! That must place a different complexion on his presence here so soon after papa's death, for to her knowledge he had never set foot in the house before.

"Susan! Do you *pay heed* to Lord John," her mother advised, looking vastly displeased with her offspring. "You must forgive her, my lord, she is at the dreamy, inattentive stage of youth, you understand."

Inwardly seething, Susan made herself smile and apologise.

"And a very enviable stage that is, if I remember aright over the distance of so many years," Lord John declared, with a conspiratorial look at Aurelia — or so it seemed to her daughter.

"Pray excuse me a moment, my lord," Aurelia said suddenly. "I am obliged to speak with Speed about the serving of tea."

Susan was left to stare after her

departing back as she bore down upon their butler.

"Don't take flight, I beg you! I am quite harmless!"

Thoroughly discomfited and annoyed now, for she was sure her parent had contrived this, Susan looked back at his lordship and said, as airily as she could: "I have not the least intention of so doing, I assure you! And permit me to set you right, sir, if I may — I am not in any degree of a dreamy nature. I was merely a trifle surprised that you should have known of my existence for so long when I must confess I had never so much as heard your name." If this was her future step-father before her, she wanted him to realize now that she had been in no way prepared for it.

"Had you not? Well, that is not to be wondered at, I daresay," he said, further adding to her suspicions. "Mothers do possess a regrettable tendency to put one to the blush, do they not?" he went on sympathetically. "My own does it to me, even now."

"Indeed?" Susan acknowledged with

some scepticism, thinking he was being very devious now and trying to ingratiate himself with her at the expense of her mother.

He smiled, and this time it was borne in upon her how remarkably attractive this rendered his face, in particular the eyes, which she noticed were very dark, with just a hint of wickedness in their depths.

"You think me too old to have a mother, I collect?" he said in rueful tones.

"No," she retorted, with far too little forethought, "merely too *bold* to be put to the blush by anyone."

Appalled by her temerity she waited for a well-deserved set-down, but his lordship was laughing delightedly.

"*Touché*! A capital sally. Putting me in my place and proving most effectively that far from being dreamy you are as sharp as a razor! I see I must tread warily in future. Tell me, Miss Gillow, do you write — verse, perhaps?" he asked disconcertingly.

"No, that is, not *verse*," she floundered, startled into confession, "but I must own to an unsuccessful venture into novel writing."

"Ah!" he said with satisfaction. "But why unsuccessful? Although I believe it is monstrously difficult to discover an appreciative publisher for the most worthy tales."

"Good gracious, sir, you are quite out!" cried Susan, sorry to have given such a misleading impression of her feeble efforts. "I have scarcely put pen to paper. Indeed, to own the truth, I have quite despaired of alighting upon a suitable theme. It is the fashion, I understand, to unfold some family scandal — altering the names to some fanciful titles and transposing the setting to a wildly romantic shore — but as a family we appear to be sadly lacking any such helpful affairs."

"That could prove a hazardous under-taking for anyone to contemplate, I fancy." Lord John's glance strayed to Lady Eleanora, some distance away. "But surely you don't entirely lack material?" he said in a low voice. "I would have thought that lady's romantic story might have inspired you."

Before Susan could fully comprehend the remark, he went on. "Not quite of the *Glenarvon* order, I grant you."

"Oh, have you read it? I should so like to lay hands on a copy."

"So you shall then," his lordship said promptly. "I will arrange for mine to be despatched for your perusal. I must warn you I found it a dead bore myself, even though I can claim a slight acquaintance with some of the protagonists. Lord, how she can rattle on — three volumes and a new character on every other page! But I see I am disappointing you. As a fellow novelist you may indeed find it invaluable."

"On how not to proceed, I collect?" Susan responded, dimpling despite herself.

He gave her a long searching look, which even without the quizzing glass she found hard to withstand. "Well, yes. But I suspect perhaps, without being too depressing of your undoubted talents, that you are not wholly suited to the business."

"Oh, I am sure you are in the right of it!" Susan agreed readily enough, thinking more guiltily than ever of her so-called novel which was suspended after one solitary paragraph — and upon which their whole discourse rested.

"Pray understand I do not decry your skills — far from it — but the prime requisite of the fashionable novelist is *secrecy*, Miss Gillow. The tale must be nurtured clandestinely, kept even from one's closest kin, and then published anonymously. But you have shared the secret with me already, have you not? Oh, I am not unconscious of the honour this must bestow, believe me, but I feel such candid disclosure before publication does not bode well for yours to be a truly scandalous epic to throw the ton into a tumult! Am I not right?"

"Indeed you are, my lord," she said gravely, "and I do believe I shall abandon my efforts henceforth — not without considerable relief, I may say!" she told him, glad to leave her Lord Quantock to face a completely mute future.

She found it impossible not to respond to her companion's quizzing manner, which she had never encountered in anyone before.

Her mama's low voice cut across

her reflections. "Susan, you are setting everyone in a bustle by keeping Lord John too long to yourself. Look to old Mrs Davenport, if you will — she is in need of her shawl."

Abashed, Susan hastened to do her bidding, but she was beyond reason cross that she had fallen into the trap of seeming to fawn upon Lord John — in the selfsame manner as all the other females in the room.

# 5

AFTER attending to Mrs Davenport's needs, and at the same time withstanding a good deal of foolish raillery from the old lady about eclipsing her mama and enslaving all the gentlemen, Susan returned to a rather forlorn-looking Camilla, who was reduced to leafing through some song sheets lying on the pianoforte. As if to support Mrs Davenport's remarks Timothy Etheridge and Jermyn at once bore down upon the girls, Jermyn being quite oblivious of the black looks cast in his direction by Mr Etheridge, as he assumed — if he considered it at all — that the latter's interest must be directed towards Camilla since they had sat down to dinner together.

"You were quite right about Lord John, Susan," Jermyn said, instantly reverting to his, and seemingly everyone else's favourite topic. "Not a trace of starch in his manner. Why, he even admitted to a fault in his driving," he went on in wondering tones, "although *that* was doing it a bit brown — wouldn't you say so, Etheridge?"

Timothy was in no mood to agree with this whippersnapper Tubb — who was, he noted, already on Christian name terms with Miss Gillow: being several years Mr Tubb's senior, with Oxford behind him and a respectable degree in his pocket, not to mention a season on the town and one hunting with the Old Surrey, all combined to give him an unshakeable conviction that he was a match for any high-mettled Corinthian who might cross his path, let alone this young chub. The spotted handkerchief which he sported during the day instead of a cravat was proof enough to anyone who was up to snuff that he was in the high-kick — although he had to allow Mr Tubb had not had the benefit of seeing that yet.

"Far from it, my dear fellow," he said loftily. "It's asking for trouble to drive a shying horse as leader, and then forget to put the mope on his face!" He gave a deprecating laugh. "Can't imagine being such a sapskull meself."

"He did say he had little choice in the team available, and the *groom* forgot the mope after most particular instructions," Jermyn said in mitigation of his lordship's lapses. "Although he freely confessed his own responsibility. Dashed bad luck, all the same."

Susan, who had been addressed initially, enquired, not without a hint of irritation: "*What* precisely was bad luck?"

"Well, the case was this — the leader took fright at a gaggle of geese just as they dipped over the crest of a hill, and he ran away with the phaeton. Imagine being able to bring a bolting team under control on a hill!" Jermyn marvelled, who had never done more than tool their curricle and pair of docile old chestnuts about the London parks. "The horse lamed himself and Lord John was compelled to drive the rest of the way unicorn."

"Nothing to that when you're used to handling a lively team," Mr Etheridge put in, surprising Susan with his comparative garrulousness, although she attributed this to the masculine horse-talk rather than his determination to outdo Jermyn on every count to impress her.

"No, I suppose not," said Jermyn, duly chastened.

Having thus gained the ascendancy Mr Etheridge asked: "Will there be dancing later, Miss Gillow?"

"Capital idea!" Jermyn exclaimed, for dancing was something he did excel at — even his sister said so.

" — I realize, of course, that it may not be thought fitting in the unhappy circumstances," Mr Etheridge concluded, in a voice redolent with sensibility.

"I would have to consult mama," Susan replied in dubious tones. "She has said nothing on the subject."

"If we do," Camilla intervened quietly, "I should be pleased to play for you."

"No, I wouldn't hear of such a thing!" Susan told her. "You must take the floor with us if we are to have a respectable number of couples stand up — there will be few enough dancers in this decrepit gathering, goodness knows! But if they are to have cards, which I feel certain they are, I cannot see why we should not have dancing. Leave it to me, I will approach mama tomorrow," she promised then.

The tea tray was removed and sure enough the card tables were set up shortly afterwards: Susan and Camilla were disinclined for cards and preferred at this early stage of their acquaintanceship to talk and come to know one another better. Mr Etheridge, quickly perceiving this and feeling unequal to an entire evening of verbal sparring with Mr Tubb and the ladies, clapped him heartily on the shoulder, said he was sure he was an old dog at the billiards, and carried him off before he could utter a word of protest.

When the two girls had been chatting for some time Camilla said diffidently: "I do hope you will not think it an impertinence in me to ask — but have you an understanding with Mr Etheridge?" She had been an acute observer of that gentleman's behaviour earlier, and knowing her brother pretty well, did not need to be told he too was already captivated by their cousin: consequently she wanted to be able to hint him away if there was a prior attachment between Susan and Mr Etheridge.

"Lord, no!" disclaimed Susan. "If he takes your fancy *I* should not stand in your way," she said encouragingly, misunderstanding the motive behind the enquiry.

Camilla denied any such thing, blushing hotly. "I — I daresay I shouldn't say so but it is my belief Jermyn is developing a tendre for you."

"I'm sure you must be abroad there. Why, you arrived only yesterday!" Susan protested, endeavouring to look suitably astonished, although she had not been unaware of some of the looks he had bestowed upon her at dinner.

It was not the first time she had been the recipient of such smouldering glances — Mr Etheridge had embarrassed her greatly on various occasions throughout the summer with his particular attentions, but with Jermyn it was different — she liked him.

As for Mr Etheridge, it was not merely that he was of a taciturn nature in her company — and therefore conversation with him was strenuous and awkward — but when he did speak she found him too tenacious of his opinions, and he gave the impression of one who would brook no argument on any matter.

Jermyn, on the other hand, was good nature personified and possessed no hint of arrogance in his manner. Besides, she had not wholly recovered from seeing her imaginary hero suddenly before her in the life and, if Mary's speculation were true, in the guise of her intended husband. Even if her sister's idea of an arranged marriage was mere juvenile fantasy — and she was not at all convinced on that head — there was little doubt in her mind (or Camilla's evidently), that Jermyn was far from indifferent to her. However, she had no experience in the art of flirtation and was probably refining too much on what were insignificant attentions.

As she was talking idly with Camilla she remembered Lord John's enigmatic reference to Lady Eleanora: what could he have meant by 'her romantic story'? She would have liked to have asked Camilla but felt she could scarcely do so. Her fancies, nourished solely on an endless diet of novels, supplied all kinds of possibilities: elopement . . . illegitimacy — Jermyn as the elder of the two children might be a nobleman's or even a Royal's son, Camilla being the legitimate offspring of Mr Tubb. She tried to think if they looked very alike. But that wouldn't mean a great deal, she decided, thinking of the variation in looks of her own brothers and sisters.

She hazarded one probing artless remark.

"I'm sorry your father was not able to accompany you," she told Camilla. "I hope he is well."

"Oh yes, but he's always so monstrously busy — posting hither and thither for his stupid clients."

"Clients?"

"He's an attorney, didn't you know? Deadly dull."

"I suppose it must be," Susan agreed, deciding elopement must be crossed off the list of possibilities: dreary attorneys, of all people, were not the stuff that abductors were made of. That left illegitimacy: Lady Eleanora had been seduced — by someone already married perhaps? she wondered, her imagination fired now — and the sober Mr Tubb had saved her from permanent disgrace

. . . *Two* illegitimate children were not to be thought of — rarely occurring even in novels — so Jermyn was the one endowed with mystery in Susan's eyes. She wished she had had a London season: there she might have learned the truth from someone indiscreet, or if not, a startling similarity with one of the Royal dukes might have been discernible at least.

As it was, her only source of information might be Aunt Selworthy. Susan recalled how ill-behaved she had been when Lady Eleanora arrived, but one never knew with Aunt Selworthy — that might have been perfectly ordinary conduct. In any event, Susan did not want to hear her undoubtedly disapproving comments on the affair if she *did* know. She would ask Edwin when he returned — she was tolerably certain he would be acquainted with the story, and would be the most likely one to tell her. However, Edwin himself was something of a mystery at the moment: she had overheard some of the guests speculating upon his absence, and her mama could only put forward the flimsy excuse of his pressing business affairs in town. Surely he would come back soon, rather than stand accused of offering an affront to some of his closest friends?

In the meantime her imagination had a free rein where Jermyn was concerned, and she looked at him with renewed interest in the days that followed.

Not that the gentlemen were there for a vast amount of the time: during the day they were outdoors for the most part, and the ladies were left to their own devices — which were not in the main of a wildly exciting nature, and the time hung heavily. Whilst the men were up betimes, breakfasting early, often leaving the house as soon as it was light, the ladies did not break their fasts until eleven o'clock and some, having trays sent up to their bedrooms, did not put in an appearance until past noon.

So, it was the early afternoon before Susan could contrive to have a private word with her mama upon the subject of dancing.

Aurelia hesitated a moment and Susan, thinking she was shocked by the suggestion, said quickly: "I'm sorry, I daresay I should not have raised the matter."

"No, no, my dear, it is not that — I was merely reflecting that there are scarcely enough of you young people to make up a set, and was wondering how matters might be rectified ... Perhaps your numbers could be augmented by issuing some invitations in the neighbourhood for one particular evening. Nothing which could be dignified by the name of *ball*, you must understand, just a few couple for a musical evening and a little country dancing."

Susan's brow had cleared, and she expressed her gratitude. "Camilla and Jermyn will be beyond reason pleased when I tell them."

Aurelia smiled thoughtfully at her daughter. "It is a great delight to me to see you and your cousins doing so well together. I have looked forward to this day for an age." She sighed and then went on: "I think I need not have fretted over Edwin's absence — in the event Lord John is well-fitted to give a guiding hand to Jermyn if such is needed, and I have his word he will look to him when they are out hunting. Oh, nothing overt, to make the boy look particular," she assured Susan hastily, seeing just a hint of resentment in her eyes. "His lordship already has taken the sporting arrangements into his own hands. I really don't know what I should have done without him on this occasion. He is charming, is he not?" she appealed to Susan, who had little alternative but to agree in the circumstances.

But Susan did allow herself to add a lighthearted warning: "I daresay he's a shocking flirt."

"Doubtless he is," Aurelia concurred, amusement in her eyes. "But even the most incorrigible flirt has been known to settle down and marry sometime, you know."

Susan would like to have pursued this subject further, but a party of ladies drifted into the room, uttering cries of satisfaction at finding their hostess, and the *tête-à-tête* with her mother was brought to an abrupt end.

"Aurelia," said a breathless Mrs George Davenport, their principal spokeswoman, "we have been on a voyage of discovery, and in the orangery we have found your archery targets. Do you suppose they could be set up in there for a little practice later?"

"Why, of course," agreed Aurelia, who, although she would not have dared to put forward a suggestion that her guests should shiver in the damp orangery for hours on end, was delighted at the prospect of any occupation beyond the customary gossiping, sewing and letter-writing.

Whilst the matrons went into ecstasies at being granted permission for their play — just like a pack of silly schoolgirls, thought Susan disdainfully — she informed her parent she intended taking Camilla for a ride about the park.

" — And you will not forget to issue those invitations, will you please, mama?" she reminded her, before quitting the room.

The gentlemen had been out shooting that day, and there was much good-natured banter over dinner when it was discovered the ladies had been practising their archery. Lady Eleanora had fared the worst, hitting the target but once, and achieving the only actual damage of the day — a shattered flower pot: Aurelia was by far the best, which was scarcely surprising as she had been quite adept at the sport some years earlier.

"Four golds?" repeated Lord John, visibly impressed when he heard his hostess's achievement. "And I bagged only a brace today!"

"Our target is mercifully still — I daresay that has something to say to it," Aurelia countered modestly.

"We could easily put it to the test. What say you to a contest — ladies versus the gentlemen?" he addressed the company.

"What — shooting pheasants, Deville?" ejaculated an outraged Sir Anthony Burns.

"No, no, an archery contest — when the weather is not fit for venturing out, of course," his lordship qualified, seeing a marked lack of enthusiasm on the gentlemen's faces.

"A regular arch-duke, ain't he?" observed Mr Etheridge under his breath to Jermyn. "Never heard such a totty-headed notion!"

Susan, who overheard this pungent

comment, was inclined to agree with Mr Etheridge for once: she suspected his lordship of fabricating excuses to stay at her mama's side as much as possible.

The suggestion was left at the mercy of the elements — ladies hoping for storms: the gentlemen putting their trust in fair weather. Since it needed dire weather, indeed, to keep them from their hunting — a hard frost which skinned the hounds' pads being about the only circumstance which could impede them in the smallest degree — it seemed that in early November an archery contest was not likely.

Looking up the huge dining table, over the glinting silver and past three branches of candles, at the sea of still unfamiliar faces about her, Susan could not believe that scarcely more than a sennight before she had been contemplating a winter of the deadliest boredom: now, with a lively evening's entertainment to anticipate and Jermyn's company, she did not mind if the gentlemen were out most of the day.

"I expect you are skilled at the archery, too?" Jermyn said to her with a rueful smile. "I have never even tried my hand at it."

"Indeed no — there was a great craze for it some years ago when mama took it up, but I was too young to handle the bow very well."

"In that event I will be bold enough to challenge you when the time comes."

"And meanwhile *I* will repair to the orangery every day to practise!"

"Wretch!" said Jermyn, with an easy laugh.

He had had a good day's shooting, with one more bird to his credit than Lord John and two more than Mr Etheridge — who, in typical fashion, claimed to have been exercising the greatest concern of them all for the stock of pheasants in the Reibridge woods: even though Meshaw had assured them there were ample birds that season. Jermyn's success had served to bolster his confidence and, as he was quick to learn by example, already his neckcloths were a little less extravagant and the more startling items in his wardrobe were doomed to stay there.

Susan could not take her eyes from her

new-found 'hero', which meant she was forever encountering his admiring gaze, causing her to blush and look away quickly. With Mr Etheridge glowering jealously in the background, it was all very heady stuff for one who had hitherto had few dealings with the opposite sex.

"Looking forward to a good run with the hounds tomorrow, eh, Tubb?" Mr Etheridge cut in when he considered Jermyn had basked enough in his paltry shooting successes.

"Yes, indeed," responded Jermyn, with more enthusiasm than Susan would have thought possible only the day before: but now he had seen the mount that Lord John had selected for him, and felt it would suit very well.

"There's nothing you can't get over with a fall, is there?" Mr Etheridge observed with appalling heartiness.

"I prefer to get over without a fall myself," Jermyn retorted loftily.

Later when the gentlemen joined the ladies in the drawing-room, Aurelia insisted to Susan's annoyance that she should play whist.

"You must partner Lord John," she

said firmly to her daughter, "and Jermyn and I intend to beat you hollow, do we not?"

Jermyn, still somewhat in awe of his lordship, although after their day's shooting not so much as he had been, smiled uncertainly and said he would do his utmost to oblige her ladyship.

Susan's vexation at being thrown together with Lord John was in some degree mitigated by Jermyn's presence: her mother was, she was tolerably certain, making up a 'family' party to see how they would all deal together. She was vastly encouraged by this when she thought about it a little more, because if she were to marry Jermyn it would not matter greatly should Lord John become her step-father: she would not be long at Reibridge Place in any event.

Cheered considerably by this reflection she allowed herself to be much more cordial towards Lord John than she had at first intended; which was not, as she soon discovered, difficult at all.

# 6

LORD JOHN, on this occasion, was correctly dressed for the evening and still managed to make every other gentleman look a trifle dull and outmoded, or overburdened with rings, fobs and seals: no hint of colour relieved the black coat and pantaloons, and white waistcoat — unless the brilliant fire-flashes from a single diamond nestling in the folds of his snowy cravat were to be counted.

However, in Susan's partial eye, Jermyn could not be faulted. He had coaxed his crisp curls into the Brutus style, which in her view suited him vastly better than it did Lord John, who also affected it, and enhanced his already handsome looks. Lord John, she decided dispassionately, as he dealt the cards, could not be called handsome, although she had thought him so on first acquaintance; the features, on closer scrutiny, were a little irregular: the jawline somewhat heavy, and the mouth

. . . She was just concluding there was a hard uncompromising line to that when he smiled at her, and said gently:

"Your play, partner."

Flustered, she apologised and turned her critical gaze belatedly to her cards.

After the first rubber, of which two games out of three went to Aurelia and Jermyn, refreshment in the form of a special punch created by the late Sir Henry Gillow was brought in. It was, as Susan knew from experience, a deceptively powerful potation, the prime ingredients being champagne and Madeira. Feeling convinced that Lord John and herself were losing solely because of her lack of skill and concentration, her consumption of the drink was scanty: Jermyn, on the other hand, recklessly took another glass whenever Lord John did so. This might have been due to the fact that he was hanging on his lordship's every word still, and was oblivious of everything else.

"Yes, I have travelled Stage," Lord John admitted in answer to Jermyn's last question, and gratifying him with this confession, "but not since my schooldays."

Encouraged, Jermyn became more expansive. "We would have travelled Mail, I daresay, but they leave at eight in the evening, as you know, and my mother did not want to travel by night — *and* you can only take a portmanteau with you." Here the two gentlemen exchanged understanding smiles at the universal female inability to travel without a fourgon-load of luggage. "In any event I could not have travelled outside on the Mail, which was what I particularly wished to do — but they are much quicker, and safer, I collect?"

Lord John raised an eyebrow. "I'm not so sure upon that point, you know. Perhaps Lady Eleanora was right not to put her trust in night travel. Did you not hear of the recent mishap which befell the Exeter Mail?"

Jermyn shook his head and waited expectantly.

"It was this way," Lord John began, putting down his empty glass, which an obliging footman replenished together with that of an absorbed Jermyn. "When the Mail was approaching the Pheasant inn at Winterslow — which I know very well, incidentally — the off-leader was set upon by what was at first thought to be a large dog. And, as the landlady of that splendid hostlery has a Newfoundland, it was a natural enough assumption in the darkness. But, to the astonishment of the coachman it was seen to be a lioness!"

Jermyn was not his only listener now: Aurelia and Susan broke off their own mundane conversation.

"What happened to the horse?" Jermyn asked, draining his glass in an abstracted fashion at one gulp.

"And the passengers?" Aurelia added, with her own priority of concern.

"The passengers fled into the inn forthwith — and who can blame them? — leaving the coachman and guard with his blunderbuss to deal with the problem. They received help from an unexpected quarter, however — the landlady's dog, which attacked the lioness and drew it from the horse!"

"A lioness in Wiltshire?" Susan said in disbelief, suspecting he was hoaxing them.

"Oh yes, Miss Gillow," Lord John replied earnestly. "The west country is very wild still, in places, you must know. They are not indigenous, of course, but lions thrive quite well there, I collect. Many's the time, when I have been staying at Badminton, the Duke of Beaufort has complained bitterly of the scarcity of foxes thereabouts — all due to the depredations of the lions in the neighbourhood."

This was said with such perfect gravity that even Jermyn looked doubtful for a second, but he smiled appreciatively when Aurelia said:

"Really, sir, that is very wicked of you! I almost believed it myself! Where *did* the beast come from?"

His lordship looked quite affronted. "To the best of my knowledge it was tracked to one of their well-known lairs on Salisbury Plain."

Jermyn's smile faded uncertainly again, and Susan, whom Lord John had been trying to bamboozle in the first place, observed in measured tones: "One cannot help wondering, can one, how they continue to prosper with all those mammoths close by at Stonehenge."

"No, I confess that same point had me perplexed for some little time," his lordship acknowledged without hesitation. "But one must remember the lion is very fleet of foot — a good deal more so than the mammoth, in any event. Not that there has not been the occasional accident — the odd unfortunate lion has been discovered completely flattened into the turf. It happens to horses, too," he added, and here the first hint of humour touched his eyes. "Such incidents are much better known, because in that case it is the local custom to commemorate the unhappy event in chalk on the hillside. Perhaps you have never seen the white horses of Wiltshire?"

Unable to withstand this nonsense any longer and with her annoyance quite dispelled, Susan laughed delightedly.

Jermyn's vacillating smile returned but was quickly removed again when Aurelia said drily: "I believe it is your turn to shuffle the cards, Jermyn."

His lordship looked saddened by this levity, but he merely sighed and took up his cards.

Susan also examined her hand with as much composure as she could muster, but was unable to resist just one more glance at Lord John: their eyes met and she was rewarded with a look of appreciation and complicity which quite destroyed her peace of mind for the rest of the evening. She resumed earnest contemplation of her cards in slightly shaking hands, but she saw nothing, only that smile, and was conscious of nothing but the violent beating of her heart.

So, in spite of Jermyn being just the least bit disguised on Sir Henry's punch, he and Aurelia won the second rubber as well.

"I can see," said his lordship in resigned tones at the conclusion, "that I had best confine my gaming activities in this house to schoolroom spillikins in future."

With great deliberation Jermyn shook his head. "Wouldn't recommend that, my lord," he advised confidentially and a trifle pot valiant. "They play a devilish high game of spillikins up there, take my word."

"They do? I am very much indebted

to you for your timely warning."

"Tell you what, you could do with a spot of practise, I daresay. How about a game now?"

"No, Jermyn, we can't play a childish game like that here," cut in Susan, alarmed he would make a fool of himself.

"Why not?" he countered belligerently. "*You* needn't play — asked his lordship," he said, fixing his unsteady gaze upon that gentleman.

"Go and fetch them from the schoolroom, there's a good girl," Lord John requested Susan.

She hesitated but a glance at her mama, who nodded, sent her reluctantly on her mission. 'Good girl, indeed!' she fumed to herself.

When she returned, Lady Eleanora and Aunt Selworthy were amongst a few other spectators who had left their own diversions at Jermyn's insistence.

Lord John opened the box.

"But this is Jack-straws, is it not? Unless my memory fails me completely." He looked enquiringly at Susan.

"Oh, yes. I'm sorry! I must have picked up the wrong one in my haste.

110

But it will serve well enough, I fancy." It was no mistake on her part: she had brought Jack-straws because it was a simpler version of spillikins — played with straight pieces instead of hooked and irregular-shaped ones. In Jermyn's condition she thought it would be easier for him.

But Jermyn was not appreciative of this concern apparently. "His lordship particularly wanted spillikins to practice," he said, frowning at Susan disapprovingly.

Lady Eleanora regarded her son with a mixture of surprise and apprehension: she did not realize how much he had imbibed that evening.

"Never mind, these will fadge just as well," Lord John said cheerfully, tipping the ivory sticks in a heap upon the table. "Shall we play so that each person continues drawing out straws until he disturbs the rest?"

Jermyn agreed. "Much better than alternate tries, ain't it?"

They cut cards for the first player and it was Lord John.

By the time he had removed six straws successfully interest had begun to mount:

Jermyn blinked first at his opponent's face, and then at the large but deft long-fingered hands. At twelve the little group gathered around began to be silently augmented with others, and by the time his lordship removed the twentieth stick there were as many onlookers, and all seemed to hold their breath. A combined groan broke simultaneously from their lips as the heap collapsed at last.

Jermyn looked dismayed. "Dash it, I didn't know anyone could take that many in one try. I can't beat it, can I?" He slumped disconsolately back in his chair, chin resting on his crumpled cravat. "There ain't enough left . . . "

"How many are there, Miss Gillow?" Lord John asked.

"Four dozen, I think. There were fifty but to my certain knowledge two have been lost."

"There you are then, Tubb, there are eight-and-twenty at your disposal — more than enough for victory."

His opponent looked doubtful about that, but nonetheless set to work with a will.

In spite of the total hush which fell

upon the company, he was able to remove only two straws without further subsidence.

"Damn!" he said violently. "You rocked the table — must've done!" he accused Lord John.

"Jermyn!" admonished a shocked Lady Eleanora in an undertone, but was ignored.

Lord John similarly ignored the imputation levelled at him by his young opponent, and went on to remove twenty more with no apparent difficulty; and the last six, scattered on the table, could have been picked up by the clumsiest player with ease. But before Lord John could do so Jermyn swept them to the floor crying:

"And you said you needed practice!"

The pieces were retrieved from the floor by an appalled-looking Major Welton who, with a wary eye on Mr Tubb, placed them back on the table.

"Sheer luck," Lord John said soothingly. "Come, let us try alternate turns this time."

"No point is there? It was you who needed the practice, not I." Jermyn was surly now, and Lady Eleanora, aware at last what was amiss, threw an imploring look at his lordship.

"True, but it's a childish game, don't you agree? I'd rather try my hand at billiards any day. What say you to a game?" Without waiting for a reply Lord John stood up.

"Excuse us, ladies, if you will."

With the least possible fuss he soon had Jermyn on his feet as well and, a friendly arm across his shoulder, they steered a steady course towards the door.

Aurelia was already diplomatically arranging another four for whist from the spectators, and had enlisted Lady Eleanora, Sir Anthony Burns and Major Welton as replacements, because Susan, thoroughly discomfited by the recent scene, begged leave to be excused further cards.

Mrs Selworthy followed her niece to the sofa, and Camilla, who had been a silent spectator also, squeezed unobtrusively onto the end beside Mrs Selworthy.

"Well now, what is one to make of that disgraceful episode?" Agnes Selworthy said with relish and total disregard for Camilla.

Susan, looking very unhappy, said: "I did try to stop Lord John but he would play the wretched game. It is my belief he wanted to pull ridicule down upon Jermyn's head before the whole company — although for what purpose I cannot hazard a guess!"

"Oh no, my dear, you are quite out there," Aunt Selworthy replied, her small deep-set eyes widening in her plump face. "His lordship did everything in his power to prevent Mr Tubb's deplorable behaviour but to no avail. How could it be otherwise? When gentlemen are the worse for drink it is beyond anyone's capability — even Lord John's — to save them from the consequences."

Camilla was seated bolt upright, and staring with passionate interest at the nearest whist game: her burning cheeks were the only sign that she had heard anything of this interchange.

"He was not really the worse for drink," Susan retorted crossly, because she knew her aunt was right — but she still thought Lord John had gone out of his way to draw attention to poor Jermyn.

"I think he was, just a tiny bit, Susan, or he would not have behaved like that, you must know," Camilla interposed quietly, causing Mrs Selworthy's head to swivel round on her short neck like an owl's. "But it doesn't really matter, does it?"

"Doesn't matter?" echoed the outraged Mrs Selworthy. "I'm not wholly surprised, of course, to hear such lamentable sentiments on your lips, miss! It is all of a piece and only to be expected from that quarter." She sniffed, and rummaged in her reticule for a handkerchief. "Hm, it's gone. I must fetch another, I suppose. No," she said to Susan, rising stiffly to her feet, "I do not expect anyone to wait upon me in this house." She made her long-suffering way to the door.

A glance at Camilla revealed that her lower lip was quivering.

"Pay no heed to Aunt Sniffworthy," Susan told her in rallying tones. "I never do. If she weren't complaining all the while she wouldn't be happy." Nonetheless she was aching to ask what

116

all *that* had been about, but the silly name served its purpose and Camilla managed a smile, so she hastily changed the subject.

"I have been meaning to ask you this age — since you lived in London — did you see the Princess Charlotte on her wedding day?"

"Oh, indeed I did! It was the most fortunate circumstance. As you know, the ceremony was in the evening at Carlton House, and the Princess drove there through the park from Buckingham House. We were admitted to the entrance hall there and saw everyone leave."

"Her dress sounded magnificent," said Susan, who like every other lady in the kingdom had pored over the descriptions in the newspapers.

"Oh, it was — white silk and silver lama embroidery! She looked like a princess out of a fairy tale."

"I cannot believe it cost ten thousand pounds, all the same."

"You would if you had seen it — and the brilliants she wore! A wreath on her head, drop-ear-rings . . . "

As Camilla chattered on there was

no doubt, thought Susan, that she had succeeded in diverting her cousin, but her own mind still drifted back remorselessly to the earlier events of the evening. She wondered, too, how Jermyn was faring: on two successive nights now, he had been carried off unwillingly to play billiards . . .

However, Lord John had not, on that occasion, led Mr Tubb to the billiards-room but directly to his bed-chamber; whither his lordship's valet, Pilton, was summoned and given instructions to put the young gentleman to bed.

The next morning was wet but there was a hunt fixed for that day, and none was deterred from joining it by the prospect of a mere soaking.

Susan and Camilla occupied their time inspecting each other's wardrobe, both of which, they decided, lacked variety.

"I shall be so glad when I have been presented next spring," complained Camilla, "and can dispense with these insipid white dresses."

"But that one is beautiful." Susan indicated a worked muslin and sarsenet evening dress lavishly trimmed with ribbon and patent net.

Camilla wrinkled her small nose. "Mere novelty, you know. I think *yours* are so much nicer than mine, but then I haven't been wearing them all year, have I?"

"Neither have I, as it happens," Susan reminded her with a half smile. "We were in mourning most of the time."

"Oh yes, I'm sorry . . . Will you be having your come-out next year?"

"I hope so."

"You sound uncertain."

"Perhaps . . . But then wouldn't *you* be, if your mama was making sheeps' eyes at the first eligible bachelor who visits us after — after papa's death!" Susan cried in a sudden bitter outburst.

"I wouldn't go so far as to say she was, well, throwing out lures exactly, but they do seem to make a perfect couple, that is undeniable," remarked Camilla cautiously.

"There, you see! You have noticed it too. I would not mislike it quite so much but they are so *flagrant* about it!"

"I don't suppose it is their intention to be," Camilla pointed out reasonably.

"But if they are meant for each other . . . " She let the sentence hang romantically in the air.

Susan did not trust herself to comment at that point, and Camilla went on: "In any event, what difference would that make to your season in town? Indeed, you might be launched at the Anlaby Mansion — imagine!" Her eyes shone at the very thought.

"There is not the smallest reason for me to imagine it, as I wouldn't go."

"Oh," said Camilla, disappointed, for she had already seen herself invited to a glittering assembly held for her cousin at the magnificent Piccadilly house. "Why not?"

"Because I don't care for Lord John and his ways. If my mama marries again she will have to leave this house, which is Edwin's, but I am not compelled to go with her. I shall stay with my brother, he would not mind, I am perfectly sure. He will need someone to entertain for him, and we shan't have to worry about the children, mama will take them with her," she said, ruthlessly disposing of everyone's future in a few words.

"I see." Camilla paused to digest this: if she entertained any doubts about the accuracy of her cousin's independent plans she did not express them. Instead she made a practical suggestion of her own.

"Well then, you had best come stay with us in the spring. Mama would be delighted to chaperon you, I am sure. It would be much more fun being together, would it not? I shall ask her at the first opportunity," Camilla declared, warming to the idea with every word.

Susan was a little taken aback at this outcome of her remarks, but it was soon borne in upon her that it would mean being near Jermyn. "Yes, that's a famous idea! And it is most kind of you to make such an offer ... But wouldn't Lady Eleanora think it a trifle odd — I mean it is not as though mama has *refused* to chaperon me next year," she admitted reluctantly.

Her cousin considered this for a moment. "No, but you haven't a town house at the moment, have you? And we have, so what more natural? In any event, it can do no harm to ask, can it?"

So, it was agreed that Camilla should broach the matter with her mama when a suitable moment presented itself . . .

Later that morning the girls went down to the deserted library, where they had taken to spending their time when they could not go out riding. They each had a book open before them, but it was a mere formality: they still found a great deal to talk about.

"When will the gentlemen return from their hunting?" Camilla asked presently.

"Not much before three at the earliest, I would hazard," said Susan, glancing at the tall windows. "The rain stopped some time ago."

"It can't be more than one o'clock," sighed Camilla.

"And I'm hungry," Susan announced. "Shall we have some nuncheon and then take a ride?"

Camilla brightened considerably upon hearing this proposal, and they started to make their way to the Blue Saloon, where Speed presided over an extensive cold collation at that time of day.

Their way took them across the vast flagged hall and they hurried to prevent the cold striking up through the thin soles of their morocco slippers, but their rapid progress was halted abruptly.

Speed was not in the Blue Saloon but by the entrance doors with a footman: also there was Lord John, whose commanding figure Susan noticed first, and with him two of their grooms. Her eye had just travelled to the supine figure at their feet when Camilla cried:

"It's Jermyn!"

# 7

UPON hearing the ladies' voices the prostrate figure eased himself up onto one elbow and looked dazedly about him.

"I'll g-get up now — walk upstairs to change — be as right as a trivet in no time."

The two ladies hung anxiously upon every word, but Lord John rapped out: "Lie down, sir!" in such a peremptory tone that Susan thought he might have been addressing an erring gun-dog.

Jermyn sank back again, and did not seem altogether unwilling to close his eyes.

"He has been thrown, has he?" asked Susan in a voice of great trepidation: on the last occasion she had seen a hurdle carried into the house the body of her father had been stretched upon it.

When Lord John nodded in an abstracted way, Camilla ventured apprehensively: "Is he badly hurt?"

"Nothing to fret about, ma'am," Lord John assured her. "A damaged leg and a bit of shaking, as far as one can tell, but if we can carry him to his room he can be examined more thoroughly."

He gave instructions to the grooms to take their burden up the stairs, bade Speed summon Pilton to Mr Tubb's room at once, and then turned his attention briefly to the girls once more.

"I will speak with Lady Eleanora as soon as I have changed out of my dirt. In the meantime if you should see her, say nothing which could put her anxiety on the full stretch — merely that we have returned a little early."

Lord John, who was not quite as mud-soaked as Jermyn, but certainly had lost his pristine immaculate look, gave the ladies a rather curt-seeming bow and turned upon his heel.

The cousins exchanged rather stricken glances.

"*Was* he badly hurt, do you suppose?" Camilla asked.

"I have really no idea," Susan answered helplessly, thinking of Jermyn's pale face.

"We ought to tell mama, surely? She would want to know."

"No, it is best not to say anything, as Lord John suggested. Everything will be done for Jermyn — we are used to falls in the hunting season. If a doctor is needed he will be fetched from Reigate."

"Doctor? Do you think he has *broken* his leg?"

"I fancy not — he did not appear to be in any severe pain," Susan said briskly, talking herself out of anxiety as much as her companion. "Come, we cannot stand here for ever, I think we should eat as we planned."

"Oh, I couldn't face a morsel!"

"Yes, you can," Susan told her firmly, although her own appetite had suffered something of a check.

Only Mrs Selworthy and old Mrs Davenport were in the Blue Saloon when the two cousins went in; and since these ladies had their heads together and were oblivious to anything beyond their plates and their gossip, it was no difficult matter for the newcomers to keep their news to themselves. In fact, after a few murmured exchanges,

Camilla and Susan sank into a worried silence.

The Blue Saloon, like almost every other apartment in the Elizabethan house, was a spacious but gloomy apartment, and the two pairs of ladies were separated by about twenty feet, the older couple being on a sofa with their backs turned to the cousins: at the end of a quarter of an hour they seemed wholly unaware of the girls' presence.

"Who d'you say?" Mrs Davenport's voice echoed querulously across the vast empty-looking room: only one motionless footman was in attendance.

"Lady Gillow, of course," responded Agnes Selworthy louder than was necessary, due to growing exacerbation with her slightly hard of hearing companion.

"Oh, ay, thought you must," Mrs Davenport acknowledged, with a complacent cackle.

Susan lifted her head at hearing her mother's name, looked at Camilla and placed a finger to her lips.

"It's no surprise to me, I may say," Mrs Selworthy went on smugly. "They were as thick as inkle weavers even before Sir Henry appeared upon the scene. That's not to say there was ever anything improper in their relationship," she added at once. "Even now they are behaving with every propriety," she allowed generously.

"Remarkably constant fellow to wait all that time, I must say," observed old Mrs Davenport with grudging admiration. "Will he get his reward now, would you say?"

"Without a shade of a doubt, in my view, but there won't be any announcement yet awhile, mark my words," she declared with total conviction. "*I* could never have brought myself to consider another man after Mr Selworthy passed on, of course, however many years had gone by."

Both girls by this time were riveted by this conversation, but Susan's one desire was to escape before Aunt Selworthy realized they were still there. She made a sign to Camilla that they should leave and, placing their plates silently on their chairs, they tiptoed out.

The footman, who would have had to

be stone deaf not to overhear everything that had passed, assisted the young ladies' departure by walking over to Mesdames Davenport and Selworthy, and enquiring with the utmost solicitude and rattling of dishes if he could help them to some more of the ginger cream or caramel custard.

"There, I *was* right, wasn't I?" said Susan in a distressed voice, as soon as they had left the Blue Saloon behind them.

However, more than the confirmation of her fears — which she had not really doubted — she was upset by the revelation that Lord John and her mama had known each other for ever. Although even that circumstance had been adverted to by his lordship when first she had met him, as she now recalled.

"Well, yes, it does seem so," admitted Camilla. "But I must own *I* would not object greatly to Lord John as a step-father," she observed, puzzled by her cousin's attitude. "They can be absolute monsters, you know. Remember the one in *The Wronged Countess*? — he was quite beastly."

Susan's eyes flashed. "I think Lord

John is quite beastly at times! Look how he treated Jermyn last night — and the unfeeling way he spoke of him today!"

This served to remind them both of the accident.

"I *do* hope he is all right," Camilla said, then apparently reaching a sudden decision she added: "I must go to mama, whatever Lord John recommended. I will see you in the drawing-room before dinner."

Left with several hours to fill before she need change, and not wanting to face the other female guests, Susan took refuge in the schoolroom for a while.

Mary and Henrietta, with Miss May, were grouped around the small fire sewing. Unless it was bitterly cold, a fire was never kindled in the schoolroom until after noon. Susan remembered how welcome that warmth had been, and how often she had suffered a scold for putting her feet on the fender.

She was greeted at once by a complaint from little Henrietta.

"Our Jack-straws have gone, haven't they, Mary? Someone has *stolen* them!"

Miss May protested at this bald

accusation, and Susan quickly explained what had happened. "I'll bring them back to you later," she promised.

"Grown-ups playing Jack-straws — that's silly," Mary commented in scathing tones. "Why, only Henrietta plays with them these days," she said loftily.

"Lord John was practising — I daresay he will be challenging you to a game soon," Susan improvised, wryly avoiding the truth about that unfortunate scene.

"Oh good," piped up Henrietta. "I like Lord John."

"He has been to see you, has he?" Susan asked, surprised.

"'Course not — we went down to the drawing-room to see him," Mary answered importantly. "Mama asked us. I liked him, too. He told me what to do about my freckles."

"He did?" Susan exclaimed.

"Oh yes. Rainwater three times a day. I think it's working. Look!" She put up her thin face for inspection.

"Well! I believe you may be right," agreed Susan diplomatically, trying to sound impressed: after all, rainwater couldn't do any harm — unlike some of the evil concoctions Mary had tried in the past. "You will be transferring your affections from Jermyn to Lord John, I collect?" she said, grave-faced.

"Oh no!" Mary denied in shocked tones. "He's much too old — he must be as old as mama, you know. I think *she* should marry him. I'd like him as a step-father. Hetta would, too — we decided."

Susan, still unused to Miss May as an ally, was nonetheless grateful for her intervention at this point: she was weary of having this self-evident fact repeated to her wherever she went.

The conversation was kept to more innocuous subjects subsequently, but as Susan was leaving she did tell the girls they might be seeing more of Jermyn in the next few days.

"I believe he has sprained his ankle in a fall, so he may be confined to the house for a while."

She hoped that was all he had done, and if it were so it would at least mean she too would see him more often — and when Mr Etheridge was not forever at her elbow.

Timothy Etheridge was very much in evidence, however, when she entered the drawing-room later: she had heard nothing of Jermyn's condition in the meantime, and had by now imagined him to be suffering every possible injury. So it was with less pleasure than usual that she saw Mr Etheridge talking to Camilla, and making a quiet cose with her impossible.

" . . . I was entered to hounds at a very early age: can't be too soon, in my view — Ah, here is Miss Gillow!"

Both their faces brightened, Susan noticed, upon her approach: poor Camilla had a particularly wan aspect. However, Susan had seen that Lady Eleanora was present and seemed cheerful enough, so perhaps it was Mr Etheridge's presence rather than Jermyn's absence which Camilla found discomposing.

Wasting no time, she asked her cousin about her brother's condition.

"It does not seem his injuries are of a serious nature — he sustained a sprained leg and a slight concussion. It was not thought necessary to seek advice."

"I should rather think not!" cried Mr

133

Etheridge. "If we horsemen called upon the faculty every time we took a toss, the wretched fellows would be run off their legs in no time."

Ignoring this hearty declaration, Susan asked Camilla if her brother would be down for dinner.

"I believe so, it is certainly his intention."

"You know, I'd dare swear that was no concussion," the incorrigible huntsman went on. "Tubb was fuddled this morning, I suspected as much from the moment the hounds threw off. It was a large field and he nearly got ridden over at the start. Just as well Maberley — master of the Old Surrey, y'know, Miss Tubb — wasn't there! He would have been in high dudgeon at such a pretty piece of work," volunteered the now-irrepressible Mr Etheridge: Susan wished vehemently he would sink back into his customary tongue-tied state.

"I would prefer to hear *his* version of events, I thank you," Susan told him in her most crushing manner.

Hitherto she had not really noticed his features, but now she decided he had a disagreeable weasel-like look about him.

"Here he is!" exclaimed Camilla, and went to greet her brother, who had just hopped into the room supported on a crutch.

"Do you excuse us, Mr Etheridge," Susan said with a sweet smile, and pointedly followed her cousin.

Mr Etheridge seemed quite prepared to ignore this heavy hint, if indeed he had noticed it, but was finally deterred from joining the cousins when he saw Lady Eleanora and Lady Gillow also moving their way: he looked around for some fellow Nimrod with whom to discuss the day's run.

Jermyn, already feeling conspicuous enough for his taste, was not best pleased to be surrounded by a bevy of solicitous females.

"Yes, yes, thank you, I'm as sound as a roach but for this dashed leg," he said impatiently.

"Dear boy, do sit down," implored his flustered parent.

"No, I'd far rather stand, thank you, mama," Jermyn told her bleakly, not relishing the prospect of being assisted to his feet again by half of the ladies present.

After expressing their sympathies at some length, the two matrons finally departed.

"How came you to take a fall?" Susan asked him.

"I was *thrown*," he replied with some emphasis. "It was over a rasper and I had the misfortune to land awkwardly, that is all. I was not the only one, I may say," he protested indignantly. "I would have gladly rid home but Lord John insisted I should be carried. There was really no call for such a great pother. Frankly, the casualty which hurt me most was the ruination of my new leathers."

Lord John made his entrance at that moment and, surveying the company with his glass, picked out the incapacitated younker and walked across to him.

After greeting the two ladies he enquired very civilly how he went on and, colouring up slightly, Jermyn hastened to reassure him.

"I am exceedingly relieved to hear that, I may say, for I would have had her ladyship to answer to, had it been otherwise. However," he continued, eyeing the injured limb critically, "try to rest that leg as much as possible or you may yet suffer a protracted incapacity," he advised quite kindly, but Susan still had the sensation his lordship was endeavouring to give the impression Jermyn was an incompetent greenhorn who needed constant supervision.

"You must excuse me, I believe Lady Gillow is trying to catch my eye," Lord John said presently, and quit the young people.

Mr Etheridge, on the watch for just such an opening, came up to them.

"Well now, Tubb, it don't look too promising for you to sport a toe next Friday, eh?" he said, in tones which could only be called gloating. "Dashed painful, I daresay," he added as an afterthought.

Susan, who had quite forgotten the coming dance, felt dejected upon hearing this, but Jermyn maintained stoutly that a few days would see him as lively as a cricket again.

Later that evening it appeared to Susan that Sir Anthony Burns was making a determined push to cut out Lord John: he had quite monopolised her mama who was, she thought with distaste, doing her utmost to make his lordship jealous.

Lord John, thus momentarily at a loose end, came over to talk to Susan.

If she had any fleeting doubts as to what they would talk about, they were quickly dispelled.

"Ah, Miss Gillow," he said, with the smile which rendered him irresistible to the entire opposite sex. (But not to me, reflected Susan, at once on her guard). "I thought we might discuss at length the fascinating fauna of Wiltshire — a subject we merely touched upon last night. Why, we never so much as mentioned the rhinoceros, I believe?"

He raised a quizzical brow at her, and resolute though she had been to treat him with not one jot more cordiality than courtesy demanded, she found herself returning his smile, and quite disarmed by his manner — which, to one accustomed to the solemn Gillows, was undeniably refreshing.

"No," she replied, falling in readily with his bantering tone, "but then we would not, for surely everyone knows the only survivor died of old age last March?"

"Now there you have the advantage of me, I confess. But the news comes as no great surprise — no indeed, for he escaped originally, you know, from a menagerie on Ludgate Hill in the seventeenth century."

Susan acknowledged this further gem of information with a half smile, then said seriously: "Was that tale of a lioness true in the first place?"

"Every word — vouched for by the *Morning Post*, no less. I wonder you did not see it as you have such a consuming interest in wild beasts."

"Then where did the lioness come from?" she persisted.

"A menagerie, ma'am," he admitted, and had the decency, she noted, to look a trifle sheepish. "Rather more recently than did that poor old rhino!"

"I have only ever seen one menagerie — in the Tower of London and a pretty shabby affair I thought it — even at the tender age of ten," Susan confessed. "Certainly there were no lions."

"Well then, we must remedy that when you are in Town in the spring — the Exeter Exchange is a far superior collection."

Susan did not care for the paternal condescending tone in which he said this: besides it suggested he had discussed her future with her mama. "I am no longer ten years old," she pointed out rather insufferably, "and fancy I shall have a vast number of more interesting entertainments during my first London season."

"Forgive me!" he said with exaggerated contrition. "I do not doubt for a moment you will. I am persuaded that with your looks you will take the Town by storm."

"Now you are quizzing me again!" she protested crossly.

He looked quite shocked. "Indeed, you do me a grave injustice, ma'am! I would never jest over such a matter with a lady. Nay, I meant it." With a look of dawning comprehension, he went on: "I see it must be the very deuce having a Beauty for a mother, but you should not let it cloud your judgment. Your dark colouring is all the rage now — just as your mama's fair looks were fashionable in her youth."

"Take care, sir, I shall most certainly *not* believe you if you dub me the Gillow Beauty!" she warned him drily.

He shrugged his broad, impeccably clad shoulders. "These things are a matter of fashion, and what one generation calls beautiful is often incomprehensible to the next. A generalization which does not in any way apply to Lady Gillow, though, it is true," he qualified.

Susan noticed his gaze had momentarily alighted on her mama, who was laughing at some bon mot of Sir Anthony's.

"But outward appearance is not so terribly important, is it?" he said suddenly. "Or it would be a bleak prospect indeed for the rest of us."

Feeling uncomfortable under his searching look, and at the turn the conversation had taken, she endeavoured to introduce a wholly different subject — not with the happiest of results.

"I believe you were there when Mr Tubb met with his accident today — can you tell me exactly what happened?"

141

Lord John's face darkened for a moment, then with a wry smile he said: "Yes, I could, but it would go very much against the pluck . . . Let me just say this — in my view that young gentleman is perhaps a good illustration of the fact that a little more is desirable in anyone than a handsome face. Don't look so fierce, I beg you!"

"I feel fierce!" she retorted. "I merely asked you about the accident, and you seize the opportunity to *malign* my cousin!"

"Perhaps I may be accused of traducing him," he conceded mildly, "but he led me a merry dance today. Remember, I have been held responsible for his well-being by Lady Eleanora, and I am only too well aware that by his foolish actions he could have sustained a broken head just as easily as a few contusions — and *that* is something I do not care to contemplate."

"I see," she murmured, subdued by this reflection. "I'm sorry."

"There is not the smallest need to apologise — your loyalty does you credit," he said lightly. "But take care not to be misled by an attractive outward aspect and a few fine feathers."

The subject was not laboured, and Susan and his lordship were soon deep in conversation about books they had enjoyed, their tastes coinciding amazingly in her view: Walpole, Scott and Cowper were all, it seemed, favourites of his too.

Later, Susan had to admit, albeit reluctantly, that she was as susceptible to his charm as any other female, but that did not alter the unpleasant fact that he was behaving like a step-father already. She regarded his animadversion on Jermyn to be beyond what was permissible in anyone *but* a parent.

At least it was becoming clear now what he was striving to do; by denigrating Jermyn in every way he was seeking to hint her away from her cousin. But why? she wondered.

Her mama might be behind it, for it was only young Mary who had put forward the Gothic notion that a marriage had been arranged between Jermyn and herself: if that were true why hadn't she been told of it by now? Perhaps

Lord John had been charged by her mother with the task of giving her a disgust of Jermyn — and that might have some connexion with her cousin's mysterious background. Perhaps he was not considered suitable even as a stepson-in-law by his lordship?

She would treat such strategems with the contempt they deserved; if Jermyn wanted to marry her — and she felt tolerably sure he would ask her sooner or later — that was all that mattered to her. Camilla's suggestion that she should go and stay with them in the spring now took on a new significance. For if her mama gave her consent to that, it would surely bode well for her relationship with Jermyn.

# 8

CAMILLA lost no time in putting before her mama the proposal that Susan should come to stay with them in town for the season. Lady Eleanora, taken wholly by surprise, was at first inclined to reject the idea out of hand, but on further consideration thought perhaps it would do no harm to consult Aurelia.

Being an unsupported hostess to about three dozen guests and their myriad dependents was no easy matter, as Aurelia was discovering: consequently she was one of the earliest risers in the house, and available at all hours to solve, as far as she was able, the many and varied problems which seemed to beset her visitors. In the space of a few days these had ranged from a maid who had thrown out a rash, as sudden as it was startling, to a mislaid diamond bracelet — mercifully discovered soon after, by the frantic owner, to have concealed itself unaccountably in one of her long kid gloves.

Aurelia was alone in her boudoir, however, when Jermyn's mother discovered her there the morning after his accident.

"Eleanora, how nice! Although I do not scruple to say I hope you come with no plaguy problems for my attention. I have had two already placed before me this morning," Aurelia greeted her lightly, but then looked conscience-smitten. "Pay no heed to me — is it Jermyn? How does he go on today?"

"No, Aurelia dear, I promise I bring no thorny matters for your unravelling. As to Jermyn, the last I heard of him he was trying to ease himself out of bed. I rather think he has stiffened alarmingly, but otherwise is stout enough, thank heaven."

"That is indeed a relief, but what sorry luck it was for him!"

"Maybe, but it is my belief he brought it down upon himself. Lord John did not actually say so to me, of course, but I have the impression he behaved idiotically — not to put too fine a point on it. I hope he may have learned his lesson at so slight a cost."

Aurelia smiled. "I suspect he may not regard being compelled to spend his time house-bound with my daughter as any cost at all!"

"No, there is a particularity in his behaviour where Susan is concerned, I fear. But at eighteen he will fancy himself in love with nigh every girl he sets eyes upon, I daresay. It probably does not signify."

Aurelia looked thoughtfully across the small snug room, furnished only with a pretty walnut desk and two or three chairs, at her friend. "And it if does signify, would you mind? Pray don't hesitate to say if you do," she added at once. "You may understandably have a much more brilliant match in your eye for Jermyn than Susan, who although she has a not inconsiderable endowment at her command could in no way be said to be an heiress."

"Such an important decision must ultimately rest with Berkeley, of course: but for my part I would be delighted to see him married to Susan. It seems to me she possesses a natural good sense beyond her years . . . Yes, in many ways it would be a most welcome match to us both, I fancy. You see," lady Eleanora went on, dropping her voice confidentially and looking a trifle uneasy, "although, as you know, I was cut off without a shilling after my marriage, my brother, when he inherited after papa's death, insisted that both Jermyn and Camilla should want for nothing. It is my opinion he never truly disapproved of my behaviour, but had little choice in the matter whilst papa lived — a situation which made him generous to a fault later. In short, the fortune I cast aside — a step I have never regretted, I may say — is now held in trust for my children."

Aurelia, knowing something of the hardship and exigencies her friend, born into the easiest circumstances, had endured, said: "I suppose nothing can quite compensate for the difficulties encountered in your peculiarly isolated situation, but to see your children's future secure must be a great joy to you. But I confess I cannot see, in that event, why you would particularly welcome Susan as a daughter-in-law."

"I was *never* isolated, remember I had Berkeley always at my side and he has been quite magnificent," Lady Eleanora maintained, just a hint of prickliness in her tone at the least suggestion of criticism of her spouse. "As to Susan and Jermyn — well, you must have noticed that my son lacks a certain matureness of understanding and has, I fear, if not held in check, all the makings of a fribble."

"But, my dear, he is scarcely eighteen!" Aurelia protested. "All young men pass through a nonsensical phase — it is only natural." Although Edwin for one had never done so, as she realized immediately she said that.

"Perhaps, and I know it is also natural that most young women should be older in their outlook at that age . . . Nonetheless I do feel that Susan would have the strength of character to exercise a restraining and sobering influence over Jermyn if he should be led into a dissipated way of life — indeed, might wholly prevent such a lapse. Not that he has shown signs of that as yet," she concluded hastily.

"Indeed no! I think you are a good deal

too severe upon the boy, and perhaps also a little optimistic in your view of Susan as a *steadying* influence," said her sceptical mama drily.

"But you must see that if he could fix his interest with Susan now — even if they were not to marry for a year or two — it would relieve my apprehensions of his losing his heart to some scheming, shallow girl who would do nothing to temper his volatile tendencies."

"You could surely forbid such a disastrous connexion?"

"We could, of course, but what purpose would that serve were they to . . . to *elope*?" She pronounced these final syllables with some effort.

"Eleanora! You are not prey to the fear that *eloping* is hereditary, are you?" Aurelia asked, obviously amused by the thought.

"No, not that precisely," her friend replied, in far from happy tones, "but don't you see how difficult it would be for Berkeley and I to do as we ought if either Jermyn, or worse, Camilla, took it into their heads to abscond? Sole control of the trust for the children rests in my hands — my brother stipulated it should be so."

"Yes, I do see it would place you in an intolerable situation but there is not the least sign that I can discern that Jermyn is likely to elope. *I* think you refine too much upon the poor boy's minor youthful weaknesses. It is quite understandable, but wholly unnecessary, I am sure."

"I expect you may be right," Lady Eleanora owned with a rueful smile. "You see I have never mentioned this to anyone before, not even Berkeley, and I think it has assumed nightmarish proportions in my mind. I feel better already for discussing it, I declare!"

"I am glad of that. You know you may trust me with your confidences, I hope."

"Yes, I do, my dear, and I cannot tell you what it means to me after all these years." Her voice trailed away, then she roused herself and went on: "There *is* one other matter I have to broach with you, and although it is in no way a problem I am not at all certain how you will view it."

"Pray go on — you begin to alarm me!"

"No, no, it is not in the smallest degree alarming, but our girls have been hatching a scheme between them, it seems . . . Camilla asked me if Susan could come and stay with us in the spring, so that they could be presented together."

"I see," Aurelia said, after a moment's surprised silence. "And whose notion was that, do you know?"

Lady Eleanora shook her head. "Camilla merely pointed out that we had the town house and it would be much more fun for them to be together — which I suppose is undeniable."

"But not much fun for you, I fancy, chaperoning two girls?"

"Oh, I should like it above all things, but *you* would surely want to chaperon Susan as she is your first girl to come out?" She paused and then said with great hesitation: "Unless, of course, there is any reason why you would prefer to be free of the peculiar ties and strains of the season in the coming year?"

Aurelia looked quickly at her friend,

smiled, and blushing very slightly, said in a low voice: "There might be, Eleanora, there might be, but I trust not everyone is blessed with such an acute perception as you. Leaving that aside, I can see one reason why Susan might wish to be under your roof — simply because it happens to be Jermyn's too."

"Yes, that had occurred to me . . . There was one further reason that crossed my mind — do you not suppose she might fear being overshadowed by her present chaperon?"

Aurelia stared. "You are not serious! I am somewhat past my first flush of youth, you know, and when I have my spectacles on look positively hagged!"

"You know very well neither you nor any *lady* would ever appear in public with spectacles on!" Lady Eleanora pointed out swiftly. "No, I shall not allow you to know anything of the matter. You are still the Lydeard Beauty in the World's view and, frankly, I think Susan might have some grounds for such fears."

"Well — I have never, ever contemplated such an effect, you must believe me," gasped Aurelia.

"Oh, I do! But nonetheless I think it a point to consider — along with many others."

"Yes, well, I don't know what to say," Aurelia admitted helplessly.

"You haven't seen our house in Park Place, it is true," Lady Eleanora elaborated, feeling it incumbent upon her to make everything as clear as possible. "We moved there only a few months ago, in anticipation of the entertaining we should be called upon to do for the launching of the children. I think I may say we live in a tolerably good style there, and it is St. James's — however, we can't boast a drawing-room of ducal proportions," she said archly.

"No possible reason why you should, is there? I am perfectly sure that if you consider it befitting for Camilla it would be so for Susan, whose portion must be so much smaller than her cousin's."

"To be honest, my dear, Park Place is quite beyond our touch, but we have hired the house for three years in the hope that by then we shall see Camilla advantageously married, and Jermyn also off our hands. After that we shall sink back thankfully into obscurity and peace in some small villa somewhere, I daresay."

It occurred to Aurelia that taking Susan under her wing might help Lady Eleanora: certain expenses could be shared and the number of guests at each gathering would be increased twofold if both families' acquaintance were invited — thus ensuring greater social success, and enhancing the girls' chances of finding husbands.

"I must own this is an idea which would never have presented itself to me, but as it has been put forward, I believe it may be an excellent plan," Aurelia said. "Always supposing you are as anxious to ward two girls as you claim!"

Lady Eleanora's delighted smile did much to endorse this, and so it was decided that their daughters should be told the scheme met with approval — if Camilla's father sanctioned it, and if nothing arose in the coming months to alter the case. Aurelia's mind now shifted to another, more personal matter, and she said a trifle diffidently: "Oh, by the by, I would deem it a particular favour if you would not so much as drop a hint to *anyone* of my forthcoming change in circumstances. It excites my astonishment that you should have guessed — but perhaps that is because we are such *very* close friends! However, the whole affair is not very far advanced, and I can see we must be even more circumspect in our behaviour than ever: I would not want to be guilty of offending against poor Henry's memory, and there are the childrens' sensibilities to be considered." Aurelia paused for a moment, and then said in a barely audible voice: "You do not consider me lost to all conduct to be thinking of marriage again, so soon?"

"Of course not, dearest! You are still comparatively young, and if there is someone who can make you happy, and with whom you wish to share your life, why ever not? Not, I may say, that *I* am the person to be applied to for guidance in such matters — indeed, I wonder that you will place your daughter in the hands of one with such a sadly dubious reputation."

"What fustian you talk, Eleanora! All that is long forgotten and, in any event, was never regarded as such a dire affair by any but the strait-laced Gillows, I'll warrant!"

"It still lingers in some minds, but I try not to regard it. Incidentally, since the subject has arisen, is *that* at the root of your step-son's absence? Pray don't hesitate to say if it is — I know well what his father's views were upon the matter."

"No, I can honestly say that he expressed a wish to make your acquaintance, but he had quite made up his mind to travel to town, and would not be diverted." She sighed. "I must confess Edwin's conduct of late has been not a little puzzling."

"Do you look for his return soon?" Lady Eleanora asked.

"No, not a word have I had from him since his departure, but for the life of me I cannot see what could be so important as to keep him in town when his own house is bursting at the seams with *his guests*."

"Might I ask if you had intended to stay at Reibridge Place indefinitely — in other circumstances?"

"Well no, I believe I would not have remained here," Aurelia admitted. "Do not mistake me — Edwin has not asked me to leave, but I felt it would be the right thing to do."

"And that has no bearing on your decision to remarry?"

"Lord no! There is the dower house, you know, and I was quite happily resigned to refurbishing it, and settling there for the rest of my days."

When Lady Eleanora had gone, Aurelia reflected that perhaps it was no bad thing after all that her step-son was away: her friend would clearly be looking higher than Edwin for a match for Camilla, as she was, apparently, a considerable heiress. The estate was entailed to him, it was true, but his sole income derived from it, and she suspected it would give him no more than a competence.

Besides, it appeared that Susan on the other hand *was* considered to be a good match for Jermyn by his mother, and one Gillow connexion would surely be thought to be enough by the Tubbs. As for her own view on that alliance, she was not altogether sanguine about it:

her opinion on Jermyn coinciding with his mother's rather more than she had cared to admit to Eleanora. However, if it were a marriage of attachment, and Susan's happiness depended upon it, she thought she would probably raise no insuperable objection.

Aurelia would not have doubted her daughter's feelings had she been present when she was told permission was granted for her stay at Park Place. Susan was in transports: she was convinced the way was now open for her marriage to Jermyn — as surely it must be, if that gentleman should wish it; and, almost as important to her, it would remove her from Lord John's vigilance. It must follow, too, she supposed, that her mama was not being swayed by his lordship's poor opinion of Jermyn; which also gave her cause for satisfaction.

The latter, who had hobbled with great discomfort and difficulty the unbelievably long distance to the library that afternoon, nonetheless thought it well worth the effort when he found Susan there alone. Unfortunately, he scarcely had time to discard his crutch, and collapse thankfully into a comfortable wing chair, when his sister burst in upon them with the news.

"Isn't it *splendid*?" cried Camilla in ecstasies, when she had finished.

"If you say so," he responded, with natural annoyance at the interruption, and a predictable fraternal disinterest; but Susan's patent disappointment at his tepid answer soon roused him to a proper degree of enthusiasm. "I mean, rather, yes, by Jove! Never heard such a capital notion! But I give fair warning I shan't let anyone else stand up with Susan at our Park Place dances!" he declared playfully, and giving Susan such a warm regard she scarcely knew where to look.

"Don't be such a nick-ninny!" his sister advised him in terse tones. "You are discomfiting our cousin." A remark which did nothing to reduce the glow on that lady's cheek.

"In any event," Camilla went on crushingly, "who are you to talk of dancing? You can scarcely walk!" She had decided now he was making a great piece of work of very minor afflictions.

"Thank you for your sympathy, sister," he retorted in biting accents. "But at whatever cost in personal anguish, I tell you now, I intend to lead Susan onto the floor *on Friday* for at least two dances." Here he gave a disconcerting winning smile at his cousin.

"If she will have you — I'm perfectly sure I would not," came Camilla's swift response, this family bickering being quite mechanical between them.

"Cheese it!" Jermyn snapped. "Do you go and read some of your Minerva moonshine!"

To Susan's amazement this order was complied with without any more verbal violence, Camilla meekly taking her book to the far end of the library. Such scenes were not wholly unknown between herself and Edwin; but she could never recall enacting them before an audience, nor had her step-brother ever cast such a look of antipathy in her direction: perhaps this sort of brangling sprang from their being so close in age, thought Susan in exculpation.

The look of dislike, which had quite distorted Jermyn's handsome features, was instantly replaced by one of the utmost pleasure. It was almost an angelic countenance: his blue eyes were crinkled with a smile which revealed even, white teeth, and the whole face was wreathed in unruly brown curls (which were the envy of Susan, whose own hair, although thick and silky, lacked any such helpful tendency).

As Susan struggled to erase her own expression of disapproval, she could not help but reflect yet again how remarkably attractive a young man he was.

"There!" he said with satisfaction. "Now we may be comfortable together. Come and sit by me," he invited, holding out a hand and indicating the stool by the side of his chair.

Susan felt reluctant to comply with this request because of his rather heartless treatment of his sister, which had, she now suspected, been contrived simply so that they should be alone: but she did as he wished with a good grace, excusing his behaviour on the grounds of the discomfort he was obviously still suffering.

"Is your foot paining you very much?"

she enquired, but ignoring pointedly the proffered hand.

"It is indeed, ma'am, but with you to divert me I have every expectation of being able to forget it anon."

"I think that most unlikely," she countered in prosaic tones. "You would fare better with a little laudanum to dull the pain."

"Oh, Susan, you do disappoint me! I thought yours would be a romantic disposition not given to talk of sickroom anodynes the first time we are alone! Give me your hand," he said coaxingly. "You cannot deny me such a small consolation."

"First you must have a stool to rest your foot upon," she said, springing up to fetch one. She scarcely knew why she was being so silly — for there should be nothing she would like more than to have Jermyn make love to her — except that his manner had been a shade too volatile for her taste.

She brought the footstool, and very carefully set his bandaged leg upon it. "There, that will be much better, I daresay."

In straightening up she knocked over the crutch leaning against the table; she lunged forward to catch it, but instead Jermyn caught her arm and pulled her towards him.

"Mm, much better," he murmured into her hair, for she had averted her face. Unfortunately in doing so she had lost her balance still further, and found herself sitting on his lap in a state of extreme confusion.

"Jermyn, please, someone might come in!" Besides which she was very conscious of Camilla's hushed presence, although the poor girl was making a valiant pretence of reading.

"None of the ladies comes into the library in the afternoon, m'sister said so," he whispered, nuzzling her cheek. "And all the hunting set are abroad once again . . . idiots that they are," he added complacently, listening to the November gales buffeting the windows.

She felt it would be undignified to struggle as he had a very firm hold upon her, so she stayed quite still — and silent, for she was completely at a loss to know what one should say in such unaccustomed circumstances.

"You must have guessed my sentiments about you, Susan," he went on with great fervour, lifting her head so that she had no choice but to stare into his fine eyes. "You do like me just a little, don't you?"

"Well, yes, of course I do, but — "

Whatever reservations she might have expressed were effectively quelled by Jermyn, who needed no further encouragement than that to kiss her very thoroughly indeed . . .

"Well, well! Would that I had sprained an ankle if that is the kind of succour to hand!"

The voice of Lord John was unmistakable and, with the blood pounding in her ears, Susan tore free of her captor and stood up a trifle unsteadily.

"I — we thought everyone was out hunting," she stammered, since Jermyn did not seem inclined to make any helpful observations but was busy straightening his waistcoat.

"That, if I may say so is perfectly obvious — or so I should hope if your reputation is not to be wholly destroyed."

A rustle of paper diverted his lordship's

attention, and he lifted his glass and peered down the length of the gloomy library. "Ah, Miss Tubb, you must forgive me, I did not see you there."

He turned back to the guilty-looking pair; for even Jermyn was looking a little abashed by this time. "So, you were not completely unchaperoned as I first suspected. However," he continued, turning his attention to Susan, who was still standing awkwardly by Jermyn's chair, "I think this must be superfluous, all the same." He drew out the three volumes from under his arm and laid them upon the table. "*Glenarvon*, ma'am, as I promised, but it will be dull work, I daresay, after your more engaging pastime," he observed, eyeing Mr Tubb sardonically.

"Oh no, I am most grateful, my lord, truly . . . You are very obliging indeed, thank you," Susan said, fulsome in her attempt to make amends for the embarrassing scene.

She felt quite wretched that, of all people, Lord John had come in at that moment.

Taking the opportunity to move away

from Jermyn she went to pick up the books. "I will carry them up to my room at once, where they will be, er, safe."

Upon this lame excuse she made her exit, feeling quite unable to withstand Lord John's disapproving scrutiny any longer.

# 9

WHEN Susan walked resolutely into the drawing-room that same evening, she could not decide which gentleman she dreaded facing the most — Lord John or Jermyn. However, she had a particular reason for going directly to her mother, who was surrounded by a small group of friends; and inevitably Lord John was one of the party. At least, she noted with relief, Aunt Selworthy and Sir Anthony Burns were also there.

With a quick nod of greeting on the way, at an unhappy-looking Camilla and her defiant brother in conversation with Mr Etheridge, Susan approached the older group with a determined smile.

" — So, you look down upon our hunting country do you, Deville?" Sir Anthony was saying, as he fixed his lordship with pale blue eyes, which Susan knew could assume a deceptive ferocity: Sir Anthony was the mildest man she

168

had ever met. "Not that I blame you for that! No one can maintain it's the best in the world — scarcely Quorn or Pytchley, what?"

Lord John shrugged. "I enjoy a good run over any country, but cheerfully confess to being no Assheton Smith — there are other pleasures in life than chasing the fox." Here he favoured the new-arrived Susan with a meaning smile, which made her wish to sink. "Especially when it means riding in the teeth of a gale all day!"

"Oh, ay, we're at one there!" Sir Anthony concurred heartily. "Would that I'd had the wit to join you by the fireside today. That's where all the lovely ladies are, after all!" he went on, with a jovial welcoming wink at Susan.

She gave her attention quite happily to their old neighbour, whose raillery she was well accustomed to, and then turned to her mother.

"My dear," Aurelia said, "I vow you are quite a stranger! I hope you contrive to find some congenial occupation for your cousins and yourself?" This blithe reflection cause Lord John's lips to quiver in appreciation, and Susan's colour to rise alarmingly, but Aurelia added with jaunty unconcern: "You have been conspiring to leave home, I hear, you saucy baggage! Did Lady Eleanora tell you your scheme has our guarded approval?"

As Mrs Selworthy's eyes goggled from mother to daughter, and Lord John's dark eyebrows rose a fraction of an inch, Sir Anthony was the only listener to remain apparently unmoved by this revelation.

"Yes, mama, that is, Camilla told me," Susan disclosed, wishing their audience far away. "I wanted to thank you for consenting to the arrangement."

"What arrangement is this?" demanded an empurpled Mrs Selworthy.

Aurelia smiled, and seemed to be enjoying the general consternation a good deal more than her daughter was. "Nothing to fly into a pucker about, Agnes, I assure you. There was merely a tentative proposal that Susan should go and stay with the Tubbs in the spring, and share a London campaign with Camilla. It makes good sense in many respects."

"*Good sense!*" exclaimed her outraged

sister-in-law, who would clearly have expounded at length upon the total lack of any such quality, had not Sir Anthony's pale stare fixed upon her in a quelling fashion.

"Susan thinks so, don't you, my dear?" Aurelia said, with a complicit look, as her daughter permitted herself a quick glance at Lord John to see how he had taken the news: but his air of detachment told her nothing. "We will discuss it all later, I promise." Aurelia gave Susan an encouraging pat on the arm.

"Edwin will never permit it if he has a shred of responsibility left in him," Mrs Selworthy asseverated, rallying a little as Sir Anthony's damping scrutiny was removed.

"My step-son has nothing to say in the ordering of my daughter's affairs, Agnes, as well you know," Aurelia stated firmly and dismissively; then she turned in pointed fashion to address Sir Anthony who was now at her side. "Your sister was used to live near St James's, I collect?"

"Indeed yes, ma'am, but that was many years ago . . . "

As Aurelia and he reminisced about seasons past, Mrs Selworthy stalked away with her head in the air and on a direct course to old Mrs Davenport. This left Susan standing next to Lord John, who immediately moved nearer.

"Well, Miss Gillow, young Mr Tubb is to be congratulated on his powers of persuasion, I fancy?" he said in an undertone, and edging out of earshot of the other pair.

"If you refer to my proposed visit with them you are quite out if you imagine the idea stemmed from him!" she countered indignantly. "It was at Camilla's suggestion."

"Ah! But he turns her round his thumb with scant difficulty. Have you not noticed? . . . However," he went on in a different tone, "you may forget that little episode this afternoon — I can assure you it will not happen again."

The bland confidence of this remark took her breath away, and all manner of furious objections rose to her lips — but no further: she had to own reluctantly to a sneaking feeling of relief beneath all her annoyance at his lordship's interfering ways. All afternoon she had been troubled by Jermyn's behaviour, whilst telling herself that if he had only been a little more circumspect in his attentions she would have enjoyed being kissed by him. It was excessively galling to be indebted to Lord John in this way, and try as she may she could not find it in her to thank him for his part in the affair.

He seemed not to expect any response from her, though, and rapidly passed onto other topics.

"I have taken it upon myself to arrange that archery contest for tomorrow," he said casually. "I shall look forward to pitting my skills — such as they are — against yours."

"But won't you be out with the other gentlemen, hunting — or shooting, if the weather does not permit of that?" She was dismayed to hear he intended spying upon her in this fashion: although after the events of the day she might have expected something of the kind, she thought ruefully.

"No, indeed I shan't," he confirmed cheerfully and quite disregarding the disappointment implicit in her question.

"I know of no observance which compels me to contract a severe chill if I do not so wish."

She could not but agree with this supremely reasonable view, and soon found herself committed to join the archery party the next day — an arrangement which was viewed with the direst suspicion by Jermyn.

He had limped over to Susan the moment dinner was announced; and, quite unabashed by their earlier encounter, he innocently begged the support of her arm to the dining-room. But when she told him later about the archery contest Lord John had got up, it was plain his encounter with that gentleman had rankled, to say the least.

"The devil he has!" he cried, and a piece of Savoy cake suspended on his fork was put down uneaten: he glared up the table at his lordship.

"Pray keep your voice down, Jermyn!" Susan urged him, although the degree of merriment at the top of the table mercifully would have precluded anything less than a Shakespearean declamation by Mr Garrick being overheard.

"You see why he has done this, don't you?" Jermyn went on, with undeterred violence. "Simply and solely because *I* am *hors de combat* and shan't be able to participate! If you ask me," he said, savagely demolishing the cake on his plate, "the fellow is jealous and nursing a *tendre* for you! Not that it surprises me — be odd if he wasn't," he interpolated, with one of his warm looks at Susan. "But to be so *unscrupulous* passes all — "

"No, no!" she interrupted him, beyond measure upset by this misinterpretation of the facts. "You are quite out, there! I believe he is trying to hint you away, but in a *paternal* role, you understand?" In an urgent whisper she explained: "I have every reason to suppose he is to become my step-father in the not-too-distant future."

Jermyn, who had looked wholly unconvinced up to that point, stared at her. "You mean, Lady Gillow and he — ? Well! Knew he was a flirt — but *marriage*?"

Words failed him there, and Susan nodded in agitated confirmation. "It's true — ask Camilla! But, I beg you, don't breathe a word to anyone else. I think they do not want it spread abroad at the moment."

"I should think not!" said the high-minded Mr Tubb, casting a disapproving look at his convivial elders.

"But look here," he went on, after a thoughtful few moments mopping up his cake crumbs. "Why, then, is he hinting me away? Dash it, I may not be the son of a duke but then, begging your pardon, you ain't exactly a duchess, are you?" He frowned. " . . . I think you should know, though, that I *am* in possession of a comfortable fortune. Not that *that* has anything to say to your sentiments towards me — I know it!" he declared, running a finger round the top of his cravat and looking a trifle uncomfortable at the direction the conversation had taken. "Just thought you should be told," he concluded lamely.

Susan's mind was thrown into a tumult by this speech: she had had not the least notion her cousin was so wealthy, but this did seem to confirm her earlier suspicions he might be of noble, even royal birth — in any event, it did not appear to accord with a hard-working attorney father. But did *he* know anything of this mystery? she wondered, and looked at him under furrowed brows.

Jermyn felt constrained to speak in face of this solemn scrutiny. "Dash it, it don't count against me that I'm heir to a fortune, does it?" he protested, puzzled. "I'm mighty glad of it meself," he said defensively.

"No, of course not," Susan hastened to assure him. "It's just that, well — it scarcely seems an appropriate moment to be discussing such matters," she said in unhappy tones.

"I suppose not, but lay the blame upon *him*!" he retorted, with another black look at the unsuspecting Lord John. "I still don't see why he should disapprove so violently!"

"No, well, I cannot see why, either," Susan confessed, but fearing it had something to do with Jermyn's obscure connexions. "But let's not allow it to blight our relationship — for that, I fancy, is exactly what he would wish. Besides," she pointed out, "I do not believe mama shares his views on this matter, or she would scarcely have agreed to my visiting you next year, would she? And her opinion weighs more with me than anyone else's."

"Yes, by Jove, you're right!" He patted her gloved hand gratefully and smiled at her, with an effect she could not deny despite his untoward behaviour.

On this note of harmony the subject was dropped, although Susan was far from feeling as calm as she pretended: the whole affair she found baffling in the extreme, and their bizarre conversation had surely confirmed — in all but an actual proposal — that Jermyn had it in mind they should marry.

What was abundantly clear was that his wide-eyed admiration for Lord John was no more after their unexpected encounter in the library, and his lordship, from being able to do no wrong in his eyes was suddenly incapable of doing anything right. That her cousin had some justification for this reversal of opinion was undeniable, thought Susan during the next few days. For, not satisfied with organizing the archery contest, Lord John was forever carrying off Camilla and herself on energetic walks about the parks; rides, upon which Jermyn might have been able to accompany them now, seemed suddenly to have lost favour with his lordship.

In fact, as Jermyn pointed out with some bitterness, he seemed to be going out of his way to leave *him* with a choice of having all the matrons in the house clucking over him, or of playing spillikins with his school-room cousins: in desperation he chose the latter course more than once. However, this shabby treatment, as he termed it in his more charitable moments, galvanized him wonderfully into regaining the full use of his damaged limb; and by the time the day of the dance arrived he had discarded his crutch, and was doing his utmost to disguise the least hint of a limp.

Susan could only agree that Lord John's behaviour did look — if not exactly shabby — a little contrived, for he had quite abandoned his sporting expeditions now with the other gentlemen. Nonetheless, she spent as much time as she could with Jermyn, and every evening scarcely left his side. However, in spite of everything, she could not deny that she enjoyed her enforced hours with his lordship; laughter seemed never to be far away in his company, and she had to admit she found that preferable at times to Jermyn's intense and somewhat ardent manner whenever they were together.

Jermyn had taken to coming down to breakfast with the ladies at eleven o'clock, and on the morning of the dance, as soon as they rose from the table, he approached Susan enthusiastically with the idea that they practise their dancing directly.

"Now? This minute?" Susan asked in disbelief: she was on her way to her own room to decide which of her only two presentable evening dresses she would wear later, and if any alterations would be necessary.

"Yes! Why not? Camilla will play the pianoforte for us, won't you?" he said decisively, and not waiting for more than a meek nod in reply. "I would like to try my leg, in case I make a cake of myself in front of everyone else, you must see."

"I would have supposed *rest* would be preferable," Susan told him. "And whom do you propose we find to make up a set at this hour of the day? — Lord John, I suppose, and some of the ladies who have scarcely opened their eyes, yet?" she suggested with a mischievous grin.

"Oh yes, I daresay Deville would prove only too willing, and I'll be bound he is skulking nearby spying upon us again," he retorted unamused. "But we need no one's assistance to dance a waltz or two, do we?" All the time they were talking he was leading them towards the drawing-room.

"But Jermyn, neither do we need to practise the waltz — it will be country dancing only tonight, you know," Susan objected, suspecting now what his real motive was.

"That's precisely what *I* told him," Camilla interpolated, finding courage to oppose her brother.

Blandly ignoring her, he said: "I daresay you haven't had many waltzing parties hereabouts?"

"Oh no, they are rather frowned upon in the country — that is one of the many reasons I look forward to being in town," Susan volunteered without thinking.

With a triumphant smile he said swiftly: "Then a little practise would not come amiss, would it?" He flung open the drawing-room door and stood back to allow the girls to go in.

Susan hesitated, and looked from Camilla's face — full of apprehension at the prospect of a scene if her brother were thwarted — to Jermyn's confident and engaging expression: she had no desire to see Camilla distressed again so she acquiesced.

There was no doubt that Jermyn, with his slim and graceful figure, was an excellent dancer. As they waltzed in solitary state about the chilly apartment, the wide skirt of his blue frock coat flaring out behind him like a fan, Susan reflected that she could have found no better dancing master anywhere. For many months, due to their mourning, she had had little opportunity to dance and she was very rusty — as she told him ruefully.

Somewhat to her surprise she found he was infinitely patient with her initial faltering and mistakes; but when Camilla came to the end of the second piece,

Susan felt they should stop whilst this harmony still reigned. "There, we have had our practice! And I'm delighted to see that your leg is really on the mend — it did not impede you at all."

"No more than I, ma'am, I assure you!" he answered in dry tones. "Come, we must continue until we can waltz together without mistake or boggle whatsoever. Camilla!" He snapped his fingers at his sister as if at an ostler in an inn yard, and when the music recommenced he swept Susan into the dance again. So they continued for some time, Susan becoming completely absorbed in the gay rhythm of the music and the direction of her feet. Then, as the last bars died away, he whispered in her ear: "Magnificent! I really can't wait to show you to the world — with such exquisite grace and beauty you will shine'em all down, mark my words!"

It was nonsense, of course, she knew that, but intoxicating nonsense and exceedingly pleasant; she was enjoying herself enormously . . .

The rest of the day flew past because the young people who had been invited for the party were due to arrive between three and four o'clock. For, although they all lived within a few miles of Reibridge Place, their homeward journeys could be fraught with difficulties; if the night were overcast, and with only carriage-lamps to show their way along winding muddy lanes, they might be compelled to leave well before ten.

Susan dressed with excessive care and diligence for an occasion which was really no more than a country hop: to her, though, it marked a crowning-point in her life. It was the first gathering which she could claim as her own for a year or more, and she had been so young then it hardly signified, but tonight her partner was her future husband — and surely the most handsome man one could wish to see? Not to mention heir to a fortune, and the possessor of an intriguing past . . . She sighed contentedly and smoothed the folds of her dress, which was transparent crape with an underdress of satin — quite outmoded now, and a shade too long as she had not had time to shorten it to a daring ankle-length, due to the waltzing interlude earlier, but it had an attractive shimmering appearance which she liked. Drawing on matching white kid gloves, she gave a final glance in the looking-glass at her hair and was, for once, tolerably pleased with what she saw. She had herself contrived to draw it up in a fashionable and artful knot at the back of her head, cunningly braided with ribbon. For her mama, in spite of being a Beauty, or perhaps because of it, had no lady's maid or dresser: the most artifice Susan had known her to use was honey-water for her blonde hair. However, on this occasion, Susan sallied forth to meet her guests feeling moderately satisfied with the results of her own modest skills.

The first person to express his admiration was not Jermyn, for whom the special effort had been made, but Lord John — who, instead of making a customary impressive later entrance, was one of the few guests already assembled in the drawing-room with their hostess.

"You are in wonderful good looks, Miss Gillow, and such a delightful dress I have never seen!"

Susan thanked him as prettily as she knew how, but, bearing in mind his lordship's well-known disinterest in young females, she fancied he was being merely polite and a little condescending.

"I hope I may be granted the honour of opening the dance with you?" he went on, both surprising and disconcerting her: she had naturally assumed Jermyn would be her first partner; besides which she supposed Lord John would not be dancing at all as her mother did not intend to do so.

Seeing her hesitation, he said encouragingly: "Come, you can't mean to refuse when I have made a special push to be the first on hand to ask you. I have even disregarded the ramshackle set of my cravat, which bears witness to my unseemly haste as nothing else could!"

After such an engaging confession she had little alternative but to accept belatedly, and she wondered at once what Jermyn would have to say on the subject.

As if reading her thoughts, Lord John remarked: "If you are fretting about offering a slight to Mr Tubb I am persuaded you have no cause — I would think it unlikely in the extreme that he will be entering the lists. He was limping badly the last time I saw him."

"But he was quite recovered this morning! We — " The words died on her lips: she would not reveal they had actually been *waltzing* together or his critical lordship would doubtless ring a peal over both their heads . . .

Lord John waited for a moment, a look of expectation upon his face, but when no further word was evidently forthcoming, he said: "Not above an hour ago I heard him lamenting the fact he could scarcely put his foot to the ground."

"Oh, no!" Susan cried in dismay. "I knew how it would be! I said he should have rested it more."

"That young gentleman has a talent for bringing misfortune down upon himself — you must have noticed it by now, I fancy," he observed with an irritating smile.

Susan would have returned an answer both sharp and unwise, but at that moment the first of her guests were announced to be coming upstairs, and she had to hasten away to greet them.

Jermyn did not put in an appearance until all twelve of the young people invited had arrived. He was leaning heavily on the crutch again, she noted with disappointment, for she had suspected Lord John to have been exaggerating the disability for his own ends. Her cousin surveyed the company with such a dejected look she broke away from her friends, and went directly to his side.

"I *am* sorry, Jermyn, but — "

"I know — you told me so!" he rounded upon her savagely.

Flinching a little at the attack, she said: "No! I was about to say we will have many opportunities to dance together in the future, so it really doesn't signify this once, does it? And I did enjoy this morning." She gave him an encouraging smile, but it did nothing to banish his sulky looks.

"I see Deville is looking like the cat with the cream. He has engaged you for every other dance, I daresay!"

A little taken aback at this assumption she was nonetheless able to tell him with perfect truth: "No, of course he has not! You have not the least call to be jealous where he is concerned — I have explained why already. If he takes the floor with me it is solely because mama cannot do so with propriety yet awhile. And, I am persuaded, he cannot help himself flirting with every female in the room!" she said for good measure.

Jermyn returned no answer to this but continued to scowl at the noisy gathering. Refusing to be daunted by his low spirits, and feeling genuinely sorry for him, she led him forward to be introduced to her friends. Their vociferous enquiries and ready sympathy soon had the effect of making him feel something of a hero, and his ill-temper evaporated. One lady in particular, Margaret Etheridge, Timothy's elder sister, seemed to take his interest: with none of her brother's lean looks, she was a generously built red-head, bordering on thirty summers, and clearly far from indifferent to Mr Tubb's flattering attentions. Susan had always considered her a trifle vulgar, even though she was the squire's daughter, and she could not disguise her astonishment that Jermyn should be attracted to a female of that sort.

It did not escape Lord John's notice, of course, indeed she was beginning to realize that very little did. As he led her onto the floor for the first dance, a quadrille, he said in sardonic tones: "I see Mr Tubb is not repining overmuch — he appears to have discovered ample recompense for his immobility."

Ignoring the subtle inflexion he had placed on 'ample', she replied with very real feeling: "Yes, I am glad — I feared it would quite destroy his enjoyment of the entire evening, for he really is an excellent dancer . . . or, so I am given to understand," she added hastily.

"Now that places me on my mettle, ma'am! I promise to do my humble and senile best," he told her, with a slight inclination of his dark head, and as Aurelia struck the first notes of the quadrille.

Afterwards, she could not have said how his dancing skills compared with Jermyn's, for during that first dance two things were slowly borne in upon her mind with a sensation of mounting panic: first, she discovered that try as she might she could not raise the least jealousy over the fact that Jermyn was flirting outrageously with Margaret; and the second revelation was the reason for that total lack of feeling — namely that she must be falling in love with Lord John. Nothing else could surely account for those delicious tremors of excitement which the mere touching of their hands could inspire in her. (Jermyn's embrace, she recalled, had left her wholly unmoved.)

Her emotions were so overset that, when his lordship clasped her hand and led her off the floor, murmuring: "I could wish that the old custom still prevailed for the first partner to remain constant for the evening," she feared she might swoon dead away — although she had never done such a silly, languishing thing in her whole life.

Lord John may not have danced with her at every opportunity, but he did stand up with her three times — a sufficient number to draw interested looks from other bystanders than the ever-vigilant Mrs Selworthy. By the second set Susan had recovered her composure in some degree; but against every recommendation of her mama, who had taught her to dance, she engrossed herself wholly in the figures and evinced a complete inability to talk at the same time.

The evening passed in a dream-like way, and only when the first guests were departing did she realize she had not been alone once with Jermyn — indeed had scarcely spoken with him. However as it neared midnight and only the resident guests remained, at their cards or talking in a desultory manner, her two cousins expressed themselves well-pleased with the evening's entertainment; and to avoid any lengthy discussion, Susan pleaded exhaustion and made her excuses.

Her thoughts were in a turmoil, and she reached the seclusion of her own room with a sensation of the greatest relief. Closing the door behind her, she leaned momentarily against it, and was about to shut her eyes for a while: only then did she become aware that there was more light in the room than came from the candle in her hand.

The man sprawled on a chair by the dwindling fire lifted his head and gave a weary smile. "I hope I don't startle you, Suke."

"*Edwin*! What are you doing up here? Why didn't you join us earlier?"

# 10

STILL bemused by her own tangled emotions Susan walked slowly towards her bed and sank onto it: there, she saw Edwin's travelling cloak draped over the foot. She had already noticed that he was still in his riding gear so he must have come directly from the stables, which was odd in the extreme — she could not recall when last he had been to her room.

He was attempting to explain. "I didn't come home until past ten and it was scarcely worth changing to face the company then, was it? Besides, I was tired."

"No, I suppose it wasn't," Susan admitted, still puzzled. "But why come to me, here? Not that I am not very glad to see you," she assured him hastily. "I cannot say why exactly, but I have been prey to the suspicion for some time that something was amiss . . . is it?"

Sir Edwin ignored that and answered

194

her first question. "I merely wanted to discover something from you — and you may depend upon it it is nothing of a sinister nature."

His try at a light response did not ring quite true to her for some reason, but she did her best to match the easy manner. "Oh, and what was that?"

"I wondered how many souls I am still entertaining under my roof? If I may judge from the carriages outside tonight, half the population of Surrey, I'd hazard!"

She could not imagine why he had not approached Speed for this information. "Well no, that was misleading," she explained. "We got up a small dance — a few friends from the neighbourhood to meet our cousins, that is all." It was difficult to discern much in the candlelight, but she thought he looked hagged to death, and certainly had dark circles beneath his eyes: but the fatigue in his voice revealed his state of mind most plainly, however he might try to conceal it.

"A dance! So the merriment continues unabated, does it?" he commented bitterly.

"Mama bore no part, of course, but I am sorry if you consider it was ill-advised," she said miserably, wishing he had chosen some other night than this one to return.

But he lifted a limp hand in protest. "No, no, Suke, it's not that. I do not mean to cast a blight over your enjoyment, but I have experienced a wretched time lately and I am becoming crabbed — pay no heed!"

She looked at him in concern. "Oh? Why is th — ?" Her sympathetic inquiry was cut short.

"Who remains then, of the house-party?"

"All of them," she told him with a surprised glance, as she drew off her gloves. "They have not been here much above a sennight, you know."

He shook his head, and then rubbed his eyes. "I can scarcely believe it, but I suppose you are right! It has seemed like a lifetime to me." Sensing that his step-sister might question him further after this unguarded remark, he said, again attempting to sound casual: "I take it then, that Deville is here?"

But it was difficult, too, for Susan to discuss Lord John with indifference now, and she replied in rather strangled tones: "Yes, yes he is."

Sir Edwin gave no sign of noticing anything odd in her response however, but ground out: "I knew how it would be! Not one damn' thing has come out right of late, so why should *that*?"

Startled at his vehemence, she endeavoured once more to discover what was wrong. "What *is* it, Edwin?" she asked in troubled accents. "Did something happen in London?"

He gave a harsh laugh and stood up abruptly. "No, absolutely nothing happened in London."

He seemed to be on the point of leaving, and she wondered how she might detain him — then he checked, his hand on the latch, and said: "What time is the company abed in the general way?"

"Not yet, in any event. I retired early, and the usual set are often at their cards until the early hours."

He swore under his breath, and drew out the watch that had been his father's. Uncertainly, he looked at Susan. "I fear it is a tedious imposition, but would you object if I were to stay with you a while longer?"

"Of course not," she told him with immense relief. "Do you sit down again." She shivered and made to put some more wood on the fire.

"No, please, I must do that!" he insisted wearily. "I fear I let it sink too low."

Susan rummaged about in a drawer, found a worsted Indian shawl, draped it about her shoulders, and then joined her step-brother by the fire. "Now we may be comfortable," she said, settling into a low chair.

"I should have asked earlier, but tell me, did our unknown cousins arrive safely after all?" Sir Edwin asked, in an artificial manner quite unlike his previous remarks, and which suggested he might have been making a morning call upon a friend.

"Oh yes, indeed they did! We deal extremely, and I am persuaded you will like them all." She recalled that she wanted to consult him about the mystery surrounding Lady Eleanora's past, but somehow that seemed unimportant now: there was, she was convinced, a more urgent need to discover what was wrong with Edwin, who was behaving like a fugitive in his own house.

"I'm perfectly sure I shall," he returned absently, the bright social air quite gone: chin on hand, he sank into a reverie which looked far from cheerful.

After a few minutes' silence she felt constrained to say: "Can't you tell me what is troubling you? Please . . . "

He raised tired eyes to hers, and said in a lack-lustre voice: "It is a very commonplace story, Suke, and one for which there is no remedy. I have lost the one person in the world I ever . . . well . . . loved."

"Oh, Edwin, I *am* sorry." Her heart truly ached for him. However, if he had told her this yesterday, although she would have sympathised, she would have lacked the insight which enabled her now to feel so deeply: for she had lost her love even before she had had wits enough to realize he *was* her love. "Might I know how it happened?"

He grimaced. "Thereby hangs a tale,"

he said unforthcomingly.

"Is that why you have been spending so much time in town?" she pressed him, when he seemed disinclined to say more.

"In part." He fetched a weary sigh. "Look, Suke, it would profit me nothing to burden you with my difficulties. You are too young, in any event — and it wouldn't be fair."

Stung, she retorted: "What has age to say to anything? How old is — is the lady in question?"

"Nineteen."

"Well then!" In a more appeasing voice she continued: "If you propose to sit there — for whatever obscure reason of your own — until the early hours of the morning, do you not think it will be a great deal easier if we talk? And I cannot suppose a discussion on any other topic is likely to divert your mind from its present miseries . . . is it? Besides, in the circumstances, I consider it only fair that you *do* tell me."

"Oh, very well," he conceded, weakening. "But I must impress upon you this is in the strictest confidence: no one, not even mama — in fact, particularly mama — must have a hint of any part of it. I shall *never* forgive you if you breathe a word to a soul," he declared, in accents so grave she felt quite alarmed, and could only nod in solemn agreement.

"There isn't much to tell," he then announced, sadly disappointing his riveted audience. "I had the ill-luck to fall in love with a lady of great fortune — and every virtue — but for my pains I have been turned off as a gazetted fortune-hunter."

"Doesn't she love you?" Susan ventured to ask.

"I have every reason to suppose she does, but it is the father who holds the purse-strings — for three more years at least — and it was he who rejected my offer. Not that I can wholly blame him!" he exclaimed, acrimony returning.

"But why? Is he dangling after a more illustrious title than yours for his daughter?"

"Oh no — it is not our line that is at fault! *He* was merely a brewer, the architect of his own considerable fortune — which is to be divided solely between his only two daughters."

"What, then?"

To her dismay he put his head in his hands, and didn't speak for a moment.

"I'm dished up, Suke . . . under the hatches," he said at last, in muffled tones. Then, raising his eyes and seeing her bewilderment, he amplified upon this unmistakably: "*Ruined!*"

"But I don't understand. How can you be ruined? You came into your inheritance only months ago!"

"It's a sorry tale, and one which reflects not one jot of credit on me, but I suppose there can be no harm in telling you the whole — now that it is all holiday with me."

She did not care to speculate what he meant by *that* desponding remark, but sat quietly while apprehension grew inside her.

"You see I never expected to survive Waterloo," he began painfully. "I was in dun territory long before that, and up to my eyes in post-obits . . . That's a way of raising the wind from money-lenders on any expectations you may have from a relative's will," he interpolated for her benefit. "Dashed expensive it is too," he added with feeling.

"Papa's, you mean?" she said in a low voice, and he nodded. "Well, what went wrong? Could you not pay off your debts when you inherited?"

"By then, I was in even more desperate straits — for it was months after I had sold out from my regiment."

"Wasn't it monstrously expensive buying a commission in the first instance?"

"Indeed it was, and at that time I was resolved to quit this life in style and glory, so I chose the most ruinous way — the cavalry."

Susan remembered with a pang how proud she had been of her dashing big brother, who had become an officer soon after Bonaparte's alarming escape from Elba.

"In the event," he was saying in desolate tones, and almost to himself, "I would have done better to be satisfied with the 27th Foot — not one poor devil of theirs survived . . . But I was not, so, after resigning and with a modest sum of prize money from Waterloo, I finally returned to England and a host of enthusiastic creditors. The money seemed to vanish in days and I was once again without a feather to fly with, and still encumbered with debts."

"Then papa died?"

"Yes — and no one will ever know how I hated myself for the relief I felt when I heard the news. But I soon had my just deserts. The entire estate is entailed, and of course I was well aware of that, but I had thought to inherit a substantial sum as well. Father had always given me to understand I would be his main beneficiary, and as I knew him to be a careful man, always beforehand with the world, I had no reason to doubt my troubles were over."

"Is the estate mortgaged, then?" asked Susan, sounding knowledgeable, although she had the scantiest notion of matters financial; but she did know mortgaged estates were regarded as highly undesirable.

"Not yet," he returned succinctly. "But papa had scarcely a brass farthing of his own, only the income from the estate, and *that* has been diminishing steadily since the end of the war. Not nearly enough, in any event, to satisfy my desperate needs."

"But mama was possessed of a fortune, was she not, when they married?"

"Yes, but he has never touched one penny of that to my knowledge. He was, as you know, the most upright man imaginable, and having said he would leave Aurelia's fortune intact, he did so. For the most part it is lodged, I understand, in three per cent consols and will provide your portion on marriage, and Mary's and Henrietta's — not to mention educating the two boys and giving them a comfortable independence apiece eventually . . . So you see why not a hint of this must be allowed to reach mama's ears, don't you? How can I possibly be responsible for squandering *her* money when papa behaved in such exemplary fashion?"

Susan looked sadly at his drawn face. "When did you first meet the girl you wanted to marry?" she asked gently, wishing to abandon temporarily the hopeless subject of money.

"Soon after I returned to England. We officers were feted like heroes for a time, you know, and I encountered her at just such a party in town. I would not have chosen that moment to fall in love, but having done so it seemed to make me sanguine for a while about the hopeless state of my affairs. Then, when papa died shortly afterwards, I very rashly proposed to her."

"So, as well as travelling up to London to see her, you *were* consulting Heasley about your business affairs, I collect?"

"Yes, that was quite truthful. I have not sunk so low that I lie about everything, you know," he told her tersely.

"How did you fall into debt in the first instance?" she said, ignoring his understandable ill-humour.

"Gaming — I told you it was a commonplace story, did I not?" He leaned back in his chair, and closed his eyes. "It seems so long ago — a lifetime almost: just one evening of abominable ill-luck, I thought in my innocence, but since then it has continued unabated." A faint smile played briefly upon his lips. "When I met Catherine I was sure it marked a change in my fortune at last, but it was not to be . . . In my efforts to win her hand I turned to the tables again."

"Oh no, Edwin!" Susan cried in anguished tones.

"Well, I thought it was worth the try: if it had succeeded no one would have been the wiser. Can't you see the temptation in that?" He shook his head. "No, of course you can't! I really should not have told you," he declared wretchedly.

"I am exceedingly glad you did! I have been worried this twelve-month about you, and it is much worse not to *know*!"

"And what do you propose to do now, good fairy? Sell your best pearls to save your wicked step-brother?" he taunted her.

"Don't, please!" she begged him, greatly distressed.

"I'm sorry, Suke! Forgive me if you can, I scarcely know what I am saying."

Swallowing hard, and blinking back the tears, she made herself ask: "How much *do* you owe?"

"Twenty-five thousand pounds — give or take a copper or two," he answered, after a brief struggle with himself.

"*Twenty-five thousand pounds!*" She was aghast. "But that's a fortune! . . . Is

207

there nothing you can do?"

"Oh yes," he replied in an unpleasantly jaunty voice, which sent a shiver through her. "There are two courses open to me: I can mortgage the estates to the hilt, and that would confer on me the singular honour of being the first Gillow, in Lord knows how many generations, to take such a dastardly step. And, I may add, with precious little prospect of ever being solvent again in my lifetime — or young James's — for the rents are down to a mere two thousand pounds a year now."

When he lapsed into silence she prompted him a little fearfully: " — And the second course?"

"Oh, there isn't really a choice before me." His voice had reverted to its low desponding tone again. "Not if I take the honourable path."

She knew what *that* meant without his spelling it out: gentlemen were always expected to put a period to their existence when faced with situations of this sort, unless they fled to the Continent for a life of exile like Mr Brummell. However, she could see why Edwin could face that alternative least of all, for he would have to leave his Catherine behind. But it was stupid, she wanted to shout at him, all for the sake of a gaming debt. There must be *someone* who could help: she racked her brains ... Suddenly a possibility occurred to her.

"Listen, I beg you, don't leap down my throat, but I believe I may have had an idea."

"Now, Suke, I didn't want you embroiled at all, and I certainly don't wish you to worry your pretty head about such a sordid affair. Rest assured you will all have a roof over your heads — even if it is mortgaged! I will leave you in a moment, and you needn't — "

"No, listen, please!" she begged desperately, sensing he was very near the end of his tether, and there was not much time left. "You recall that, just before you went to London, we discussed the house-party and the possibility that mama might marry again? Well, I have good reason to think she *is* contemplating just such a step."

There was a slight flicker of interest in his features. "So? It does not come as any great surprise to me," he said dully.

Susan licked her lips nervously. "Well, no, perhaps not, but the man she is intending to marry is wealthy — very wealthy indeed — I know he is because you told me," she added in mounting agitation.

That did surprise him. "*I* did?"

"As rich as Golden Ball, you said."

An extraordinary expression came over Edwin's face which frightened her. "You don't — you can't mean — " He seemed to be fighting for his breath. " — Deville?"

"Yes," she whispered, not daring to take her eyes off him.

A maniacal laugh burst from him, as devoid of humour as it was terrifying: he laughed till tears rolled down his cheeks. Realizing he was hysterical she hurled herself at him and shook him by the shoulders as hard as she could.

"Stop it! Stop it!" she shouted.

He did so, almost as abruptly as he had started, a blank, shocked look in his eyes. Relaxing her hold, she took his hand and sank shakily down onto the floor beside his chair. There they stayed motionless and silent: she shrank from speaking again in case it should throw him into another paroxysm as inexplicable as the last . . .

After what seemed to be an age, he cleared his throat.

"I'm sorry," he said thickly.

Not trusting herself to speak or even raise her head to look at him, she increased the pressure on his hand in reply.

" . . . but you see," he went on, as if every word were an immense effort, "Deville is the man who, at the very beginning, lent me the greater part of the money."

# 11

SUSAN began to feel she could not sustain any more shocks or revelations that night — although, of course, by the time Edwin made his shattering announcement about Deville, it was already the early hours of the following morning: she had never experienced a more eventful twenty-four hours, and resolved not to complain of boredom ever again.

"Lord John is a friend of yours, then?" she asked her step-brother, frantically trying to reconcile this new information with what she already knew of that gentleman.

"He was — I doubt he counts me amongst his dearest acquaintance at this present," he said grimly.

"So *that* was why you did not want to be here for the house-party," Susan said in a ruminative tone. "And, only think, if your offer for Catherine had been accepted all your troubles would have evaporated . . . *Confound* the brewer and his grasping ways!" She gave Edwin a smile of rueful sympathy, then suddenly subjected him to a closer scrutiny. "When did you last eat?"

"Oh — I really can't remember — but it does not signify, I have no appetite."

"Of course it does!" she retorted severely. "Small wonder you are melancholic — there is nothing more lowering to the spirits than gnawing hunger."

"Suke! Do you really suppose a mutton chop will cure my problems?" he exclaimed, with wan humour.

"Well, it may go a step in that direction," she declared, and got stiffly to her feet to ring the bell.

"No! Don't summon anyone!"

She turned her head. "Why ever not? I know it is late, but one of the servants will be on hand until everyone is in their beds. You are still the master here, you know!" she told him in rallying accents.

"Maybe, but no one is aware of my presence except you."

"*No one?* But what of your horse? The stable boys must have seen you, surely?"

"No, I took the precaution of leaving Sabre at the inn."

"Well, really!" she said, disgusted. "I cannot but say that I think this has been managed in the most scrambling, underhand fashion!"

"But you see I thought I could depend utterly upon you, Suke, to keep mum about my visit, in the event of things going wrong," he pointed out in reproachful tones. " — Which they have, as even you must agree."

"If by going wrong you mean discovering Lord John's presence here, then, no, I cannot agree," she answered rashly, determined to try and keep him at home, come what may: for if he left now she was terrified she might not see him again. "He is here, but with the intent of becoming one of the family, which surely must throw a different light upon his loan to you? *Something* could be devised, I am perfectly sure, for a more good-natured man I never saw." This commendation would not have sprung naturally to her lips earlier, but she freely acknowledged now that she had misjudged his lordship in some ways.

"He would need to be endowed with an immoderate degree of good-nature to forget twenty thousand pounds — I could not ask that of any man, and certainly not of a good friend! Besides," Edwin went on disparagingly, "I do not altogether believe this tale of marriage — I think Deville came here to see me, and for no other reason. Lord, wouldn't you have come hot-foot, if it presented you with the first opportunity in a twelve-month to retrieve a lost fortune? He didn't know Aurelia, and it is not to be supposed a confirmed bachelor of his sort would get himself leg-shackled in a week — even to the Lydeard Beauty. No, he was invited as *my* old friend."

Susan had been bursting to interrupt this ill-founded notion. "But they have known each other for ever, Edwin!"

He stared at her in stupefaction. "If he has, that makes him a sly-faced snake in the grass, for he never mentioned it to me in all the years I have known him!"

"Perhaps he would not wish it to be known whilst papa was alive — not if he already loved her then," she suggested tentatively.

"I've never heard such fudge! But I don't believe it," he said dismissively, " — any of it."

Susan, standing doggedly by the bell-pull, hoping to be able to use it just as soon as she had convinced her step-brother, explained at length the various incidents and circumstances which led her to suppose a marriage was arranged — if not announced.

"Well," he acknowledged finally, "you may be right, but there's a devilish lot of tittle-tattle and speculation in it for my taste."

"Stay and see him, Edwin, please," she begged, when she saw he was vacillating a little. "It is only fair to *him*, surely? If you just walk away from here," she went on, carefully avoiding any hint as to what he would do then, "Lord John would still not have his loan repaid, would he, and it is a shabby way to treat a benefactor." She frowned. "Has he pressed you for repayment?"

"Not once: I should almost feel better if he had. He has been so damned *good*

216

about everything!" he cried savagely.

"But you will see him, won't you?" she persevered in wheedling tones.

"You don't know what you are asking," he told her, a look of total dejection on his face.

"I think I do . . . And I tell you this," she went on brutally, "if you refuse, I shall have no alternative but to think you a coward of the first water. And I do not believe you are that."

There was a taut silence while Edwin stared fixedly at the fire, and Susan watched and waited for his reply.

At last he fetched a deep sigh. "Very well . . . I see I have little freedom of choice, in the event."

"Good!" she exclaimed, and promptly rang the bell.

"Oh, look here!" he protested, but now a good deal enfeebled by all that had gone before. "I said I didn't want — "

"Well you cannot stay *here* all night," she told him patiently, "so someone in the household must be apprised of your arrival, and then your own room can be made ready."

"No call for that, I am still quite

capable of putting myself to bed!" he said in tetchy accents.

"Yes, but with the house as crowded as it is, I would not vouch for someone else not being in occupation already!"

He glared at her. "They wouldn't have done such a thing, surely?"

"Well, you did give mama to understand she must not look to see you yet awhile, did you not?" she pointed out reasonably.

"Nor would I be back had I realized I was to be bludgeoned from pillar to post in this fashion," he told her forcibly; although the tone was not wholly resentful, she was relieved to hear.

A heavy-eyed house-maid put in an appearance eventually, and made her departure some minutes later, a good deal more alert, to carry the news of the master's mysterious nocturnal return to her unsuspecting fellows.

"There now," Susan addressed Edwin, allowing herself some small degree of complacency, for she felt something had been achieved at last. "When you have eaten you must go to your bed, for I vow you look as though you haven't slept a wink these past nights." Indeed he was but a shadow of his erect, elegantly-clad self, she thought sadly.

"I do not anticipate a dreamless slumber tonight, either, I can tell you!" he declared with some acerbity. "Not if I am to face Deville within hours."

Susan did not enjoy a tranquil night herself, and in part for the same reason as her step-brother: she was not looking forward to seeing Lord John the next day or indeed ever again. Edwin's sorry tale, upsetting though it was, had affected her more deeply because it involved his lordship; their affairs, it seemed, were inextricably entangled with him, and there was little prospect of being able to put him out of her mind for one reason or another. Another cause of her disturbed night was that, in face of Edwin's scepticism, she had finally lost patience and told him to ask Deville point-blank if he did intend to marry Aurelia. She had little doubt of the outcome, but nonetheless such irrefutable confirmation would be far from welcome: at the moment she could allow herself just the tiniest hope it was not so . . .

* * *

Sir Edwin sent a verbal message to
Aurelia the next morning to inform her
of his return home, and apologize for the
somewhat furtive manner in which he
had accomplished it: to Deville he wrote
a brief note to acquaint him with the
same news and requesting his lordship to
see him in the study at his leisure some
time before noon, if it were convenient.

As he had foreseen, he himself had
slept but little, and as soon as a fire
was kindled in the study he repaired
there to await Deville. Whilst he was
confined to his father's old room he
took the opportunity to go through every
paper, document and letter left there, as
he had done times without number for
the past six months: always he hoped to
prove Heasley wrong, and discover some
forgotten investment or a clue to some
further monies which might salvage his
fortunes — always he was disappointed.

Consequently by eleven o'clock, when
his visitor answered the summons, his
dark hair was awry from much distraught
ruffling, his cravat inelegantly loosened

220

and askew; and, between these two disordered features, was a face so haggard and hollow-eyed that it was small wonder that Lord John should be visibly shaken by his host's appearance.

"Edwin!" he cried, with the utmost cordiality and before the door had closed behind him. "It *is* good to see you again!" He advanced with outstretched hand. "My dear fellow," he went on, and, concerned now, gave the wan face before him a searching look. "You're clearly unwell. What is it?"

"No, no, I'm in fine fettle!" Sir Edwin exclaimed with desperate heartiness, rising belatedly to his feet in an attempt to prove it, and extending a clammy hand of welcome. "Had a rough ride yesterday — arrived home late," he elaborated rapidly to stem further comment. "And you know how it is after a week or two toddling all over the Village — one feels as lazy as Ludlam's dog afterwards. Be glad to recruit for a day or two." Having babbled this highly misleading explanation, he realized it did not sound altogether admirable behaviour for an absent host, particularly one who was also indebted to his listener to the tune of twenty thousand pounds: at least it behoved him not to brag of recent high-living in London, he thought just a trifle too late.

Both men were dark-haired, but the resemblance ceased there: Lord John was the taller by two or three inches and more broadly built than this friend, and when Sir Edwin had sunk back into his chair his lordship towered over him. Although not invited to do so by his clearly distracted host, Deville drew up a chair, faced Sir Edwin across the desk and waited for all to be made clear.

"I must offer you my profound apologies for not being on hand to greet you when you arrived," Sir Edwin said in the same febrile manner as before. "Should have been, but for pressing legal business in town. I expect Lady Gillow told you," he went on, flatly contradicting his earlier remarks.

"Yes, indeed her ladyship did," Lord John said smoothly. "And I must confess to having enjoyed one of the best country visits in many a long year, in spite of your regrettable absence," he confided with an

222

apologetic half smile. "In my experience her la'ship is an admirable hostess, quite without equal, so you need entertain no fears on that head."

"Oh no, I was in no doubt of her ability to cope, not in the least," Sir Edwin responded, watching his lordship's face carefully, as they spoke of Aurelia, for tell-tale signs of admiration and attachment.

As if on cue, Lord John then declared: "Your stepmother has enslaved me for life — I can't deny it! No London drawing-room can boast anyone to outshine her quite extraordinary beauty, in my view . . . And, of course, those wonderful looks are merely a part of her charm. However," he went on, with a deprecating cough, and evidently feeling he had said a little too much, "I scarcely need to tell *you* what is already so well known." Sir Edwin looked up from the jumble of papers before him, with a fleeting nervous smile. "No, quite," he muttered. "Deville," he then burst out earnestly, "you must know why I have asked you to come here for a private word — that outstanding matter between us — I had to see you — should never have left it so long, but — "

His lordship cut across this incoherent outburst. "Pray don't disturb yourself on *that* count. I am fully aware how long these legal coves can take to sort out even the most unambiguous will. Rest assured I have not the smallest intention of harassing you — I hope you know me better than that."

"Indeed! You are — have been all that is considerate," Sir Edwin said brokenly.

"Nonsense!" Deville retorted, at a loss to understand his friend's excessive display of sensibility over the matter. "I have endured no hardship on your account. To be frank, I would not have missed this visit for the world, and I stand indebted to you for that alone." He smiled to himself as if over some private felicity.

Even that over-generous statement was not true, thought Edwin miserably, as Aurelia had been responsible for the invitations. He thought she had asked him on his own behalf, but perhaps Suke was right and they were old friends . . . He still did not know how to break the news of his ruination and, emboldened by his desperate plight, he tried to exploit the last, admittedly vague remark.

He cleared his throat, and said in strangled accents: "I hope you will forgive this intrusion into your own affairs, and indeed I may be monstrously premature in my surmise, but it has been brought to my notice — I had as lief not say by whom, you understand — and rest assured I would not mention the matter were it not related in some sort to . . ."

There was a merciful pause in this verbiage, and Lord John with a cock of a quizzical eyebrow remarked: "Out with it, man, for pity's sake! I shan't eat you, I promise, whatever dire doings I may stand accused of in your absence!"

Sir Edwin responded with a ghastly grin. "Oh, no! Nothing dire! Dammit, I don't know how best to put it, but, well, you needn't answer if you don't wish, of course!"

"No, I shan't! But for God's sake, Edwin, the suspense is killing me!"

His young host swallowed hard, and announced in a rush: "I believe it may be in your mind to marry into our family at some time in the near future?"

Lord John started, and fixed a dumbfounded gaze upon Sir Edwin for a full half-minute. "How the devil . . . ?" he murmured to himself. Then his brow cleared, and he nodded. "Yes, of course, I see why Lady Gillow should have confided in you above anyone else — but we did agree it should remain our own secret for the time being."

"There is some truth in it, though?" pursued Edwin, unable to reassure his friend that Aurelia was not his informant; however, he would be scarcely overjoyed to know it was the talk of the whole company.

"There is," Lord John acknowledged austerely, "but at the moment *I* am certainly not prepared to say any more. I am sure you understand?"

"Lord, yes!" agreed his embarrassed friend in considerable relief, glad to have cleared that hurdle at least. "I apologise profoundly for having raised the matter at all, but it may have some bearing on what I must tell you now. Indeed, you might wish to change your mind, in view of it."

"I doubt that," declared Lord John

unequivocally. He gave his discomfited host a look of the deepest compassion. "Edwin, am I right in believing you wish to tell me that for some reason it is beyond your power to repay that wretched loan at the moment?"

"Not just at the moment, Deville, but *ever!*" he said in despairing accents.

With unimpaired calm, Lord John replied: "Well then, you had best tell me about it."

Edwin did, only omitting any reference whatever to Catherine and his blighted hopes of marriage, in case Deville should think, with the brewer, that his intentions there had been only mercenary.

Lord John listened with great attentiveness, and only at the conclusion of the sad tale did he draw out his silver snuff box, and offer some to Sir Edwin. "My own mixture — Fribourg and Treyer." But it was refused, nonetheless, with a gloomy shake of the head. He took a pinch himself, every elegant move watched moodily by Edwin.

"So," he mused at last, dusting the snuff off his fingers with a fine lawn handkerchief, "what's to be done?"

"I must mortgage the estate — the only decent thing to do," Sir Edwin said resolutely. "I came to that conclusion last night. There's no help for it."

"Hold hard! Let's not be too hasty," Lord John cautioned. "You have been uncommonly frank with me and I appreciate that. Now, as I see it, the first and most pressing matter to be attended to is the five thousand pounds you owe to old-ten-in-the-hundred, Solomon — as distrustful and shifty a character as one would ever wish to meet with, from all accounts," he interpolated distastefully. "I will settle your affairs with him myself, when next — "

"Oh, no! I couldn't possibly allow — " began Sir Edwin, outraged.

"You, my boy, if I may say so, are in no case to disallow *anything*," his lordship said firmly. "I will redeem your debts from that unsavoury gentleman forthwith, and put a period to the interest, which is no doubt accruing at a breath-catching rate. Then, you will be indebted only to me. For the time being we will let matters hang in the hedge, and I shan't press suddenly for repayment, you need not fret." He raised a quelling hand as Sir Edwin made to protest again. "As you have discovered my thoughts of marrying into your family, I believe I shall let the outcome rest upon the successful conclusion of that marriage," he went on thoughtfully. "Yes, as part of the marriage settlement, as it were, your debt will be declared null and void. The lady, I need hardly add, will not be aware of this — unless it is your wish she should be told. If, for any reason whatever, the ceremony does not take place — well . . . " He spread out his hands. " . . . I regret the debt will stand. Then, you may well be forced to take the drastic step of mortgaging Reibridge Place, for I would no longer consider it any personal concern of mine. Do I make myself plain?"

"Yes, yes," Sir Edwin nodded vigorously, still looking somewhat dishevelled and overwrought. "But you are too generous, and I really cannot see why you — "

"I believe I may well be so, where you are concerned," his lordship interposed bluntly, allowing the first hint of criticism to creep into the discourse. "You acted like a greenhorn when you were past the age for such dangerous and expensive flights — no one to my knowledge ever recovered his fortune at the table where he lost it. Had I known of your regrettable weakness I would not have introduced you to the Nonesuch Club in the first instance, although I dare swear you would have run aground in less exalted surroundings without my help. Nonetheless, I readily accept some small degree of culpability in your affairs."

Sir Edwin found this confession hard to withstand from one he regarded solely as a benefactor, but Deville brushed aside his objection impatiently.

"There can be no doubt, whatever the root cause, that you have suffered a good deal for your follies . . . To return to your charge of generosity — no, in general I shall consider myself well-rewarded if I am fortunate enough to secure my lovely bride. Now," Lord John continued in a different tone, "I am sure I do not have to impress upon you that what has passed between us this morning is in the highest confidence. Indeed, if any breach of it should be brought to my notice I would

230

view it with the utmost displeasure, and I might be obliged to reconsider my arrangement with you." He rose to his feet and grinned. "Pluck up! We must both pin our hopes upon the nuptial knot being safely tied, must we not?"

# 12

ALTHOUGH adjured so earnestly by Lord John to keep silent regarding their private arrangement, it was not to be supposed that Sir Edwin could leave his step-sister in ignorance of the success of what, after all, had been her own suggestion. Indeed, his first thought at the termination of that fateful interview was for Susan, and on enquiry of Speed where she was to be found, he was told that Miss Gillow had kept her room the whole morning.

So, for the second time in four-and-twenty hours, Edwin trod the corridor to his step-sister's room: his approach on this occasion was markedly different, though, from the first — his step was lighter and a good deal less furtive, his appearance regaining its spruceness, and, almost hourly, his spirits were recovering their tone. The latter could clearly not be said for Susan, whom he discovered, jaded and pale-faced, in the same chair where he had left her in the early hours of the same morning.

"Suke, for God's sake, did you not go to your bed at all?" he exclaimed, shocked.

Her head jerked up when she heard who it was, but her face did not lose its strained look. "Of course I did," she said with impatience: only a man, she thought, would fail to notice that she was not still wearing her evening finery, but was in a muslin morning dress of the simplest style. She had been quite unable to face anyone as yet, and had thankfully used the dance as an excuse for her late rising. Hoping that Edwin would come to her the moment he had anything to tell her, she had nonetheless almost given up in despair, and was on the point of going downstairs when he entered. "Well, what news?" she asked, noting his improved looks with a mixture of relief and apprehension, for she scarcely knew what to wish for.

"Better than for many a long day, entirely thanks to you, I may say! Indeed, I never allowed myself to hope they could be so good again. Deville's a real trump

— I've not met his equal anywhere! I always knew him to be a real out-and-outer — but this I never expected!"

Susan felt she could do without the ecomiums upon Lord John. "Yes, but what did you discover?" Her mouth was dry, and she clasped her hands together tightly to prevent herself shaking. "Was I in the right of it about the — the marriage?"

"Yes, by Jove, you were!" he said in admiration. "But his surprise was prodigious, and he assumed it was Aurelia who had told me — but then lovers always believe everyone about them to be blind. And it was pretty plain to me, merely from the manner in which he spoke of her that he is greatly enamoured. Suke?" he asked, eyeing her anxiously. "Are you really feeling quite the thing this morning?"

She made an immense effort. "I'm still a trifle fatigued from last night, that is all," she replied; adding with uncalled-for tartness, "you did detain me till all hours, you know."

"Yes, I *am* sorry — I know I should not have burdened you with my troubles," he said, full of contrition. "But, on the other hand, I can only say it was very lucky for me that I did." He told her the whole of what had passed between Deville and himself, concluding with the solemn warning that she must never utter a word of it to anyone — particularly Aurelia.

"So, everything depends upon this marriage between Lord John and m-mama," she managed to say at last, in a leaden voice.

"Yes, but I thought you would be as delighted as I," he remarked, puzzled by her tone.

She hastened to assure him, and he looked relieved. "I was sure you must hold Deville in as much respect as I do, and will welcome him into the family with just as much enthusiasm. Good Lord!" he exclaimed suddenly, much struck. "Of course! He will be a sort of step-father to me, I suppose, as well as to you. Well, all I know is that I shall be forever indebted to him for his kindness — and to you, dear Suke, whose idea it was. Thank you," he said softly, placing a hand in an awkward fashion upon her shoulder for a moment.

This gesture of gratitude, coming as it did at the end of such a distressing speech, was almost her undoing: her lip quivered and her throat tightened, but somehow she found the strength to give him a convincing smile, and no other immediate response was necessary.

"I must go to Aurelia," Edwin declared guiltily. "She will think me irretrievably lost to all conduct if I do not mend my ways forthwith — which, I may say, I fully intend to do. I shall apply myself to the running of the estate at first, in an endeavour to render it more profitable, and," he went on, pacing about the room and warming to his subject, "yes, I do believe I may take up the law! Oh, Suke, I feel as though I have emerged at last from a long tunnel!" he cried in exultant tones.

She followed him with her eyes, an ineffable expression upon her own face. "Do you suppose then, that you may be able to marry Catherine, after all?" she asked tentatively, but her remark was sufficient in itself to extinguish his jubilation at one.

"Oh no, I think not. It would be foolish beyond permission for me to entertain even the slightest hope in that quarter, at least before my affairs are settled beyond dispute. I would certainly hesitate before I confronted the brewer with a havy-cavy tale of this sort! I can imagine his hard-headed response only too vividly!" he said in wry accents. "No, as you are well aware, young ladies are expected to marry, and I don't doubt a worthy parti will be found for Catherine before next year is out."

"But if, as you say, she loves *you* — ?" Susan felt the strongest compassion for unrequited love, now, wherever she found it.

" — that must not be allowed to stand in her way," Edwin concluded the sentence for her. "I should be a monster to condemn such a lively and attractive creature to dwindle into an embittered spinster — albeit one with a fortune at her command . . . Now, you must excuse me, I have to see Aurelia. Then, later, I should like to make the acquaintance of our cousins at last."

"Oh, yes," said Susan, rousing herself

from some exceedingly gloomy reflections. "We are in the habit of sitting in the library — Jermyn, Camilla and I, that is — you may find mama with Lady Eleanora, I expect."

"I will see you in the library, then? You are quite sure you are not indisposed?" he asked, with renewed concern.

Making a colossal effort to convince him, she sprang lightly to her feet and grinned. "Of course I'm sure, you great gaby! I am this minute bound for the Blue Saloon where I shall consume a luncheon of quite disgusting proportions — I'm ravenous!"

"Oh, I see," returned Edwin, satisfied. "You were always prone to be hipped if unfed!"

But when he had gone, she stood in a dazed fashion for some minutes before stirring. From feeling desperately sorry for Edwin the night before, she found now she was inclined to envy him: he had lost Catherine, it was true, but he was able to make plans for busying himself about the estate, and for taking up a career — all the things which were forever denied her. It was an unavoidable fact, she thought, that young ladies must marry — as Edwin had said — or their only alternative was to moulder into maiden aunts at best, at everyone's beck and call. If she herself should decline future offers on account of a broken heart, her situation, she knew, would be deplorable: residing (where? she wondered fleetingly) with her mama and Lord John; and her four brothers and sisters, until they should marry and leave home. Aunt Selworthy would stay with Edwin, she decided. Then, a most unwelcome thought came into her mind: might there not be more infant additions to the family from her mama's second marriage? But the prospect mercifully receded as she recalled something that was said after the difficult birth of Hetta, seven years ago, to the effect that her mama would bear no more children.

No, she thought, shaking herself from these painful reflections, such a future she could not contemplate: but nor at the moment could she face the thought of marriage. Perhaps she could stay with Edwin in this house? Even the prospect of Aunt Selworthy as a permanent companion did not deter her, so much did she dread the notion of Lord John as a step-father. For the moment, then, that was her resolve: as soon as the union was announced she would approach Edwin with the suggestion she stay with him. She had been able to afford him some encouragement and support, and now he could repay her perhaps, in this way; if he should demur, she might have to tell him her reason for asking, but she hoped fervently she would never have to confide that secret to anyone . . .

So wrapped up had she been in her own and Edwin's affairs that, when next she saw Jermyn, it jarred her into recalling that only the day before she was quite happily dreaming of her future as his wife: indeed, might already have been committed to wed her romantic hero if he had not hitherto always stopped short of an actual proposal.

Both cousins were in the library; Camilla reading *The Unguarded Moment*, one of the novels she had borrowed when first she arrived at Reibridge Place; and Jermyn was sprawled glumly in a wing-chair, his leg supported on a stool. There was a profound silence about the pair when Susan came upon them, of the sort that suggested to her they had had one of their brangles.

Jermyn rose to greet his cousin at once, scarcely favouring his injured limb; but after smiling at Camilla, Susan quickly enquired of him how he went on.

"I believe my leg to be finally on the mend, thank you, ma'am. Although I shall forever regret having to forego the dancing last night."

Camilla cast a displeased look in his direction. "After last night I fancy it is his *tongue* that should be in splints, do you not agree?"

Recollections of the dance came flooding back to Susan then: Jermyn talking endlessly to the overweening Miss Etheridge; her own dances with Lord John — which were the only ones she remembered with any clarity; and Camilla . . . At that point she realized with a pang of guilt she had scarcely noticed her cousin throughout the evening. So before Jermyn could return some cutting reply to his sister, she said: "I do so hope you enjoyed the entertainment, Camilla?"

"Yes, thank you, it was everything that was delightful." Her studied politeness was in marked contrast to her sisterly tones, and Susan was beginning to find their endless bickering a trifle tiresome.

"Well, I hope that means you found partners aplenty," Susan declared with forced brightness.

"Didn't need 'em with Major Welton to lead her onto the floor at every opportunity, did you, sis?" interposed Jermyn, taking his chance to redress the balance of disparaging remarks and slurs.

"I stood up with him twice, that is all!" Camilla protested, her pretty features suffused with colour. "In any event, I think him a most proper-behaved, gentleman-like man," she said pointedly, and then added in defiant tones: "I am not ashamed to say we deal very well together!"

Susan had not noticed that the bluff, rather taciturn sportsman had been singling out Camilla for particular attention, but on consideration she thought them well-suited — except in age, of course: the major must be old enough to be her father, she reflected censoriously. (But that judgement was short-lived when she remembered that Lord John was, in fact, destined to be her own stepfather.) "Yes, Major Welton is a good friend of ours," she said encouragingly to Camilla. "When you penetrate his excessive reserve, you discover him to have the most agreeable nature."

But the major had served his purpose as far as Jermyn was concerned, and he addressed Susan again. "I have not seen Deville lurking behind every *torchère* and pole-screen today — perhaps we may hope his vigilance is waning a little?" he said sardonically.

"He *is* indoors, I collect," Susan hastened to tell him; and this served to remind her of Edwin. "But I quite forgot to give you my news — my step-brother has returned and has promised to join us here later."

Jermyn expressed only a luke-warm interest, no doubt seeing his arrival as yet another check upon his advances towards herself. However, when he made Sir Edwin's acquaintance he appeared to take him in great liking, and quickly transferred the regard and admiration he had displayed for Deville to his cousin.

Susan, observing this volatility and remembering his behaviour at the dance, was inclined to be severe upon him, and judged him to be sadly lacking in steadiness of character: but then, the salutary thought occurred to her that much the same perhaps could be said of her own conduct. She had, in the space of a very short time, found her original mistrust and dislike of Lord John to be transformed into a deep respect and love; and conversely, she had been dazzled by Jermyn's singularly handsome looks into thinking he was her perfect hero, but had come to realize how shallow a sentiment that had been, based wholly upon her vague daydreams of the ideal beau. Now, she scarcely knew how she regarded him: even the mystery surrounding his birth had lost its fascination for her — if she discovered him to have been born in the purple it would make no difference whatever. Perhaps though, she thought hopefully and anxious not to be too critical, his character would show to greater advantage if he were not with Camilla all the while, and at daggers drawn.

It soon became apparent that, in any event, Jermyn's feelings towards her had suffered no real change: he was as attentive as ever, and Susan was forced to the conclusion that his flirtation with Miss Etheridge had been merely the result of pique at being unable to dance that night. Consequently, *she* was quickly made to feel the inconstant partner, and so, being for the moment unequal to contending with a spurned Jermyn, she was careful to reveal no violent alteration in her sentiments. That there was a difference would have been discerned by any close observer of the couple (and Camilla was one such), because Susan no longer followed Jermyn constantly with her expressive eyes, but reserved these looks — quite unconsciously — for Lord John whenever he was present: however, Sir Edwin, who had not seen their early behaviour, soon concluded that Jermyn was quite captivated by Susan and that she was not wholly indifferent to him.

Jermyn had been quick to tell Sir

Edwin that Susan was to stay at Park Place with them in the spring, which served to strengthen his suspicions of a future connexion there. But when Edwin referred casually to the visit the next day, while Susan and he were alone, he made no mention of these conjectures. And she, who had been taken somewhat off her guard when she had heard Jermyn refer to the visit, was quick to explain it as innocently as possible. "It was at Camilla's suggestion, you know, and at once I saw what a splendid notion it was! It will be so much more fun being together, you must see — and they live in St James's!"

Edwin frowned a little. "Has your mama given her consent to this arrangement?"

"Oh, yes! She fell in with the scheme at once. I daresay it relieves her of any tiresome responsibilities, when she wishes to devote her time to her own forthcoming nuptials."

"Yes, but I own that puzzles me a little," Edwin said doubtfully. "It seems a trifle odd in her that she should abandon you for your come-out when

— if she is to have ducal connexions — she could launch you in the grandest style imaginable, under the auspices of the Duchess of Anlaby."

"Oh, I would not want *that*!" emphasized Susan. "Besides, I expect they will not marry so soon: it is not to be thought of that they should do so before papa has been dead a year, surely? And, in any event, perhaps the Duchess may not approve the match."

"Deville will pay scant attention to *that* at his age!" Edwin said witheringly, dashing her hopes in an instant.

"No, I suppose he would not . . . But Edwin, I beg you will not try to influence mama in the matter," she entreated him. "I have quite set my heart upon staying with Lady Eleanora," she lied: her preference at the moment would have been to avoid her come-out altogether, but she knew she had to endure it, and Park Place was infinitely more attractive to her than Anlaby House for the occasion.

"I hardly can raise the matter with Aurelia, can I? Not without seeming to pry into her future plans — and, remember, we are still not supposed to have heard a whisper of her marriage." Edwin was already full of apprehension that some heedless remark might ruin his secret arrangement with Deville: so much depended upon it.

Susan smiled with relief. "No, of course I shan't breathe a word to a soul, you need not fear on *that* head."

Matters were left there, and the house-party continued as before — but with the addition of Sir Edwin in his proper position as host; and the loss of Sir Anthony Burns, who had left the morning his host returned, thus missing him completely.

But, at last, Sir Edwin was able to take Jermyn under his wing in the way Aurelia had planned he should initially, and — with Jermyn's leg quite mended now — they rode about the estate a good deal, as Edwin put into practice his resolve to apply himself to its more efficient management.

To Susan's relief, Lord John took to accompanying the gentlemen again on their sporting excursions, and so it was only in the evenings that she was thrown upon his company to any great extent; and with Jermyn continually at her side still, it was not difficult for her to remain generally aloof from his lordship. She could not, of course, avoid him altogether, and when he did succeed in claiming her undivided attention, all her well-prepared excuses to leave him dissolved, and she found herself — at the time — thoroughly enjoying her conversations with someone possessed of such wit and address: afterwards, she found the recollection of these occasions bitter-sweet, but she knew, nonetheless, she would treasure them all her days.

Once Sir Anthony had departed, one or two of the other guests began to take their leave and, two weeks after the host's return home, the house-party had dwindled almost to a family affair: Lady Eleanora had posted back to London to be with her husband, Berkeley again, leaving her children at Reibridge Place; Lord John stayed on, of course, but all the other resident guests were gone. However, most of the evenings were enlivened by the neighbouring gentlemen, like Timothy Etheridge and Major Welton, who remained after partaking in the day's sport; but then they rode home, leaving a very small company behind them.

No limit had been set upon Camilla's and Jermyn's stay, nor upon Lord John's, to Susan's knowledge, and she foresaw with some trepidation this intimate gathering stretching into December.

But then, one afternoon, when the four cousins were turning into the lodge gates for home after a pleasant ride in the pale autumn sunlight, they came upon Lord John and his man driving out. A travelling cloak concealed his lordship's stylish garb, and Susan noted with mixed feelings that he carried some luggage with him on the phaeton.

"Ah, Edwin! Well met!" Lord John exclaimed, as he acknowledged the rest of the party briefly by doffing his tall beaver hat. "It was not my wish to seem rag-mannered by taking my leave so precipitately, but I have little choice, I fear. A letter has just come to hand from my father — William, my brother, has succumbed to a feverish disorder, it seems."

"I am sorry indeed to hear that.

I trust it is not thought to be of a serious nature?" Sir Edwin said, inevitably perturbed by anything which might upset his benefactor and friend.

"It may be nothing worse than one of his putrid throats to which he had long been a martyr," Lord John told them, "but it usually takes nothing less than a calamity for his Grace to be persuaded to put pen to paper — my mother is the family correspondent in the common run of things. So you see I am anxious on several counts."

They all murmured their sympathy, and Sir Edwin said, of course he understood, and he hoped Lord John would find his brother fully restored to health when he arrived home.

Farewells were said, and Susan and Edwin exchanged raised eyebrows; then the quartet rode for a time in silence, but for the swish of dead leaves fetlock-deep about the horses' hooves.

# 13

IT was the lugubrious Mrs Selworthy who had the inestimable good fortune to find the announcement in the columns of the *Morning Post*: although the discovery could not wholly be put down to luck, being the result of that lady's assiduous scanning of the Deceased columns of every newspaper and magazine which came her way.

"Ah, I had a feeling I should see something of the sort today," she declared in a hollow voice to her niece and nephew, who were playing cribbage by candlelight in the gloom of a December afternoon.

They were accustomed to their aunt's desultory commentary, as she painstakingly read the newspaper, seated some five yards away by the fireside and illuminated by a branch of candles upon the tall stand at her elbow. Susan glanced briefly across at the pool of light, and her aunt's capped head bent over the small print, but was a great deal more interested in Edwin's counting out his score on the cribbage board, as he was nearing a victorious total of sixty-one.

Both players were quite engrossed n their own affairs until they heard:

" — Duke of Anlaby's heir, in hi. thirty-seventh year, at his house in Jermyn Street . . . "

Sir Edwin jerked up his head and met Susan's look of consternation.

"What is that, Aunt Selworthy, Deville's brother, you say?" He pushed back his chair and went over to her. "May I see?"

She handed him the newspaper with some reluctance, but was not to be deprived of her pleasure so easily. "*I knew how it would be* with that unlucky family," she said, looking across at her niece with an air of achievement. "Did I not tell you when first I heard of the marquess's belated marriage that his mother must still be prey to the greatest misgivings about the succession? There are so many ways we may be struck down in this life, let no one forget that . . . My goodness, Aurelia may not know

253

of this sad event yet!" She rose to her feet at once, and busily wrapped her shawl about her.

"But would she not have been informed by Lord J — ?" Susan began, surprised by the suddenness of the news (for she had almost forgotten Lord Grantham's illness) into an incautious remark, but Edwin threw her a swift look of admonition.

"I daresay they lack the time to write to all and sundry in such tragic circumstances," he commented repressively. "But I am sure Aurelia would wish to know at once," he added, handing the *Morning Post* back to Mrs Selworthy, who needed no such encouragement to depart with her woeful tidings.

"Will it make any difference to the marriage, do you suppose?" Susan asked her half-brother anxiously as soon as they were alone.

"I wish I knew," Edwin replied, leaning with his elbow upon the mantleshelf, and staring disconsolately into the flames. "His brother has been wed these past six months, and there may be an heir on the way."

"Yes, and it might be an heiress, which would scarcely help matters greatly," Susan put in. "From your knowledge of Lord John, would he let such a consideration as the succession to the title weigh with him in choosing a wife, do you suppose?"

"My dear girl, how should I know?" Edwin said tersely. "I have only been acquainted with a second son all these years — it would not come as the smallest surprise to me if *he* had never given this particular situation a thought before now. In any event he has chosen a wife already ... And Aurelia is still young enough for child-bearing, it is true," he murmured.

"Yes, but don't you remember there was some suggestion, after Hetta's birth, that she would have no more?"

"Good God, of course there was! I had quite forgotten. Well, that must throw a doubt over the whole business, one would suppose — unless Deville is prepared to put Aurelia before everything else," he said, beginning to pace about in a restless fashion. "I wouldn't put it beyond the bounds of possibility, all the same: he was monstrously taken with her," he added, a hint of optimism in his voice. "He may not care a groat for the perpetuation of the title — and remember, if his brother had died *after* he had married Aurelia, there would have been no altering matters, would there? He may certainly view it in that light if he considers himself betrothed to Aurelia — I cannot believe him to be the sort of fellow who would cry off if his word were given."

The unworthy thought crossed Susan's mind that her mama — if sufficiently besotted — might not have told Lord John of her inability to bear children, but she did not care to voice such a suspicion. Instead, she wondered: "If they *don't* marry for such an unforeseen reason as this, do you really think his lordship would withdraw his offer to you over the loan?"

"Oh yes — he would be bound to." Edwin was adamant. "In any event, I should insist we kept strictly to the arrangement — it would only be honourable, dash it all!"

Susan sighed. "Yes, I suppose so . . . "

She knew better than to argue once honour was mentioned. "What are you going to do?"

"Do? Why nothing, for the moment. What do you suggest I do? Rush in to see Aurelia, and blurt out the whole story, after all these weeks of secrecy — and put the entire business in jeopardy?"

"No, I see that would not be wise," she conceded. " — And to approach Lord John."

"Would most decidedly not be wise!" Edwin stated incontrovertibly. "No, we must wait and see again — and please, I beg you, still not a word to anyone about it. I must own it excites my astonishment that Aunt Selworthy has, even now, dropped no heavy hints to us — especially considering what you overheard her say to Mrs Davenport months ago," he reflected. "And you have done exceedingly well so far — and you must see at this delicate stage — "

"No, of course I shan't say anything — you may depend upon it!" Susan assured him, annoyed to be doubted.

"Oh, well, we may not be left in suspense for very much longer, I

257

suppose," Edwin said philosophically. "Aurelia must tell us sometime."

"Listen," Susan said presently, "could you not ask mama — perhaps a few weeks hence — if she will be wanting the dower house? Say you have been considering hiring it to someone, perhaps? Then she might feel constrained to tell you something of her future plans."

He gave the matter a little thought. "It might seem I was trying to oust her from this house, and I would not want to give that impression at any price. But it is something I will bear in mind, should the opportunity arise." He smiled at her. "Yet another idea for which I stand indebted to you . . . I cannot imagine how I shall contrive my affairs when you leave for town in March!" he added, only part in jest.

"Oh, I daresay all your difficulties may be solved by then," she responded brightly; and wished she could foresee a similar prospect of alleviation for her own wretchedness.

It was a week since Camilla and Jermyn had left finally, and for Susan it meant a return to her uneventful life once more — but not to the empty boredom she had suffered previously. Now she was prey to all manner of misgivings and apprehensions about her future, as she waited for her mama to take the family into her confidence. When she put pen to paper now, it was no longer to attempt to write a frivolous novel, but to scribble one of her almost daily letters to Camilla. Susan felt the need for a confidante, although unfortunately there was a vast amount she could not share with her cousin; she had thought she might be expected to play the romantic role of go-between for Camilla and Major Welton, but that relationship had not, it seemed, blossomed into love. But Camilla was more than happy to oblige Susan in a similar capacity for her brother.

However, Jermyn was due to go up to Oxford for the Hilary Term in January and, as he was a lamentable correspondent, Camilla warned her cousin that she would be in no position to supply any intelligence of that gentleman's doings until March — when, in any event, it would be unnecessary, as Susan herself would be with them in Park Place. In an ingenuous aside, in one of her letters, Camilla also gave it as her opinion that her brother would not offer for any lady at the moment, due to his going up to Oxford. Susan knew that Camilla had been sorely disappointed that Jermyn had not proposed before he left Reibridge Place, for above all things she seemed to have set her heart upon their being sisters-in-law as well as cousins: but Susan kept her counsel on the subject of marriage — whether to Jermyn or anyone else.

From time to time, Camilla also dropped hints of a degree of domestic strife at Park Place, between her papa and Jermyn over the matter of going up to university: her brother was not bookish, she reminded Susan, and was very much inclined to view Oxford as somewhere to 'knock up a lark' (as he expressed it) — much to her papa's dismay; for he, in the way of parents, cherished highly unsuitable ambitions for his heir. It was not that Jermyn was in any way a dullard, Camilla maintained loyally, but no one could deny he lacked *application* . . .

The news of the sudden death of Lord

John's brother caused surprisingly little comment at Reibridge Place: Aurelia had spoken of it to her family, and told them she would be writing a letter of condolence to his lordship. She had asked Edwin if he wished to be included, or did he intend to write himself? Relieved to be given the opportunity to avoid communication of any sort with his creditor, he somewhat ignobly allowed Aurelia to act on his behalf.

At dinner, that same day, Mrs Selworthy had indulged in a certain amount of idle speculation about the prospects for survival for the Anlaby dukedom, if the young bereaved Lady Grantham was not carrying an heir; but was silenced quite brusquely by Aurelia — causing Susan and Edwin to exchange speaking looks across the table.

After that slight flurry of excitement little reference was made again to the subject, and if Aurelia received a reply from Lord John she did not mention it.

During the short days of winter, when visiting beyond the confines of the village was impossible, Susan found time at last to read *Glenarvon*. Far from finding it a 'dead bore', as Lord John had deemed it, she revelled in the tale and even found it deliciously shocking in places; it was so very different from the tame romances to which she was accustomed. Lord John had, in a spirit of helpfulness, pencilled in the real names of some of the authoress's fictional characters: these signified but little to Susan, who was acquainted with none of them, but she could not but wonder at the dissipated conduct the protagonists indulged in — she thought it alarming, even allowing for the fact that the writer had placed them in a Gothick setting far removed (she hoped) from anything the London season might offer. Nonetheless, the novel had added a certain spice to her own coming visit to town, and she hoped she might be gratified by a glimpse of the shameless Ladies Holland, Oxford and Melbourne, and even of the heroine herself, Lady Caroline Lamb: the wicked hero, Lord Byron, she could not hope to see, as he had left the country before the book was published — and small wonder, she thought to herself.

262

When she had read the handsome volumes she was left with the difficulty of how to dispose of them — for dispose of them she must, she had decided. She was convinced her mama would not have approved her possession of *Glenarvon*, and the more she reflected upon it the more puzzled she was that Lord John should have pressed the book upon her in the first place: it was scarcely the gesture of a repressive step-father to-be. She resolved the problem to her satisfaction by placing them high up on a library shelf where no one was likely to find them: she then endeavoured — with little success — to put the disturbing story, and its even more disturbing donor, from her mind . . .

In the new year Sir Edwin found the opening he had been awaiting, and was able to ask Aurelia casually about the future of the dower house.

She was thrown into a momentary confusion, and said, seeming a trifle distraite: "Oh yes — the dower house — you are anxious to see it occupied, I daresay — quite understandably. Or is it that you are contemplating matrimony, and want me gone from under your feet?"

"No, ma'am, nothing of the sort!" Edwin exclaimed, unhappy to have the tables turned upon him in this fashion. "I thought I had made it quite plain I have not the least desire to evict you or your family from your home."

"Perhaps, but a future Lady Gillow may well hold other views upon that!" she smiled. "However, if that is not at the root of your inquiry, may I crave your indulgence on the subject of my own future plans for just a little while longer? I believe I shall be in a position to enlighten you all soon, on a certain matter," she added in enigmatical tones. "And I would hope that might be before Susan leaves for town in March, in any event."

Embarrassed, and wishing heartily he had not adverted to the dower house, Edwin reassured her and begged her to forget he ever mentioned it.

When he reported the gist of this exchange to Susan later, they concluded that, on the whole, the case looked hopeful for Aurelia's eventual marriage to Deville: it was only to be expected that the loss of his brother should have obliged them to delay making public their intentions.

* * *

It was an interminable winter for both Susan and Edwin, and even the small dinner parties that Aurelia arranged occasionally, when the lanes were fit for carriages, were anticipated with quite disproportionate pleasure at Reibridge Place. Their guests rarely numbered above half-a-dozen, and were drawn exclusively from the Davenports, the Etheridges, Sir Anthony Burns and Major Welton — most of whom were Aurelia's friends. Susan even came to look forward to seeing Miss Etheridge, who was the only other young female: which, she reflected, was indicative of the depths to which she had sunk. Many were the times when she wished her two schoolroom sisters were nearer to her in age.

There was one such gathering of neighbours in early March, and as the weather was exceptionally dark and threatening, everyone had taken their leave by six-thirty — all, that is, except Sir Anthony Burns.

Susan paid little heed to this circumstance, and assumed he had some business to discuss with Edwin concerning his estate, which marched with theirs; but then her mama suddenly spoke to them all in a curiously nervous and formal-sounding voice:

"Now that we are on our own I believe that Sir Anthony has something of import to say to you." She smiled encouragingly in his direction, where he stood talking with her step-son.

On hearing his name, he turned to face his hostess, his pale blue stare at once softened by a most affable expression. "Dash it all, Aurelia, it's *your* place to tell them, ain't it?"

"Oh, very well, if you wish it," she conceded, with an incredibly demure look. "Susan . . . Edwin . . . Agnes . . . we would like you to be the first to know that we are to be married." She did not elaborate upon this simple statement, but held up her hand to Sir

Anthony who stepped over to enfold it in a fond grip.

Mrs Selworthy was the first to recover from this staggering announcement. "Aurelia, my dear, I wish you very happy — and I congratulate you, sir, you are a fortunate man indeed! I must own it did not come as a *complete* surprise," she could not resist saying. "I did just harbour the tiniest suspicion."

Whilst Aunt Selworthy was congratulating the happy pair, Susan was sitting quite rigid and speechless by her side on the sofa, facing her mama. She cast a paralysed glance in Edwin's way, but saw to her relief that he had sufficient control of his emotions to be mouthing the correct words of felicitation, though he looked very pale.

" . . . but unlike Aunt Selworthy, I confess I had not the least glimmering that such an event was imminent!" Sir Edwin concluded, with what Susan considered must be the greatest understatement she had ever heard in her life.

"Susan?" Aurelia said gently. "Is it such a dreadful shock, my dear? I hope you may not disapprove too violently, but," she glanced at Sir Anthony, "we quite understand if you should feel overset, in the circumstances."

"Oh no, mama!" she responded much too loudly. "It is *splendid* news!" Only now was it being borne in upon her that Lord John was *not* to be her step-father after all. "I could not be more delighted, I do assure you!" She went to embrace her mama, and to receive a fatherly peck on the cheek from Sir Anthony, hoping Edwin would forgive her this display of enthusiasm: which, as she told him later, had been quite unavoidable if she were not to appear churlish in the extreme.

"Of course, of course," he then acknowledged. "I only hope my own behaviour seemed tolerably cordial and heartfelt?"

"I think you conducted yourself with astonishing address, and said everything that was proper," Susan told him admiringly. "But it does mean disaster for you, does it not?" she said, going straight to the heart of the matter.

"Yes," Edwin agreed hopelessly. "But what an amazing *volte-face* on Aurelia's part that she should hurl herself at Sir

Anthony, only months after contemplating marriage to Deville!" he burst out.

This aspect of the affair troubled Susan, too, and she tried to find excuses. "Perhaps she never really thought Lord John would marry her, and she has known Sir Anthony for ever: it would not surprise me if *he* had proposed before Lord John."

"I still think a delay of a few months even would have offered less of an affront to Deville."

"Maybe, but if he has cried off solely because of his family's desire for an heir, perhaps mama cared but little if she does offend him! But if that was the reason, it is so unfair! And what of you? Lord John cannot really mean to withdraw his offer to you merely because of it?" she said disbelievingly.

"Why not? That *was* our arrangement — and he has lost the wife of his choice, remember. I know how he must feel upon that head!" he declared with a wealth of feeling. "Well," he sighed wearily, "whatever is at the root of it all I can scarcely go to her and say why are you marrying Sir Anthony and not Deville, can I? Perhaps she simply changed her mind."

"Of course, your asking her about the dower house may have precipitated matters," Susan pondered aloud.

"And whose idea was that, pray?" demanded her wrathful step-brother, but when she started to apologize, he said: "It does not signify, Suke. I am persuaded mama would not fly into Sir Anthony's arms just because *I* mentioned the dower house to her."

Susan was frowning. "I cannot understand why Aunt Selworthy said she knew all about it, when I distinctly overheard her say to old Mrs Davenport — "

"Oh, you must know our revered relative well enough by now, surely?" Edwin interrupted. "She could not bear to be caught napping on such a matter ... But enough of that, I must apply myself to my own affairs. May was the month put forward for the wedding, was it not? And so, by then, I shall have this house to myself, and will be able to place it upon the market."

"Sell it, you mean?" Susan exclaimed. "But where will you live? And Aunt

Selworthy?" Her own difficulties of that sort had been solved, for she had no objection to accompanying her mama to her new home with Sir Anthony. However, she did not like to think of Reibridge Place being sold, even for the sake of Edwin's solvency.

"My dear girl, I cannot order my affairs for the convenience of indigent relations," he told her, with a snort. "*I* shall be compelled to seek out modest lodgings in town, and perhaps she may have to do the same if Sir Anthony does not feel any particular need of her sunny presence about him."

"Oh, Edwin!" she cried, in the liveliest dismay. "Is there no other way for you?"

"None," he said succinctly. "I suppose matters could be said to have fallen out quite well in the event," he went on in bitter tones. "If Aurelia had simply not married again at all, I would inevitably have felt more compulsion upon me to preserve Reibridge Place for the boys to grow up in. As it is — " he spread his hands helplessly, " — they will have Sir Anthony's vastly superior rolling acres in which to disport themselves."

"And so will I, but I had rather stay here!" she said vehemently.

"You? Why, you will be wed before the year is out! I'd wager a monkey on it — if I had one."

"Then you would lose it," retorted Susan coldly.

"If past experience is any guide, you are probably right," he conceded in rueful accents. "When do you travel up to town?"

"In two weeks' time . . . Oh, Edwin, I don't *want* to go away and leave you all!" she cried, suddenly stricken with a sense of impending doom.

"Fiddlesticks! Besides, you must know it is your bounden duty now to sally forth and marry a fortune, since I have shown such a lamentable talent for losing them!"

His tone was light and his intention frivolous, Susan knew that well enough, but nonetheless it sowed the seeds of an idea in her mind; which, by the time she stepped up into the family chaise bound for London, had crystallized into a firm resolve. She would marry Jermyn, if she had to propose to him herself: elopement might also be necessary if the money was to be in time to save Reibridge Place, she thought ruthlessly, permitting herself no doubts as to whether her future spouse would bestow twenty-five thousand pounds upon her for the asking.

After all, as a cousin of sorts, Jermyn was almost a Gillow himself, and even Edwin could not balk at his assistance if he were his brother-in-law as well.

Lady Gillow had decided to accompany her daughter to London, as the list she had made of commissions for Susan to purchase dress lengths, gloves, stockings and a multitude of other items, had grown to such a formidable size that it would scarcely have left Susan any time for her own considerable shopping. Besides which, Aurelia thought the visit would provide an admirable opportunity for her to see the Tubbs' town residence and the setting for Susan's entrance into Society.

So, that damp morning in mid-March, mother and daughter sat facing each other in the swaying carriage, as it floundered through the muddy Surrey lanes to London: and it was Aurelia, with her gay chatter of silk warehouses, dressmakers, milliners, Bond Street shops, balls, theatres and assemblies, who gave the appearance of an excited girl about to be launched on her first London campaign. Susan, for her part, listened politely and — feeling she alone carried the burden of the whole family's fortune upon her shoulders — wondered anxiously if Jermyn would have been changed by his time at University, and how he would greet her after a parting of three months.

# 14

WHEN Susan ventured forth upon her first London shopping expedition with her mama, it was quickly borne in upon her why Lady Eleanora always insisted that Camilla be chaperoned about the town: for Park Place — a cul-de-sac — led directly into St James's Street, in which were situated the most fashionable clubs — including White's, with its huge bow-window where the privileged coterie of gentlemen would sit with their quizzing glasses, ogling every female who passed by. (Ladies, Susan was warned by her elders upon arrival, *never* walked that way.)

She was thankful, therefore, for the protection afforded by the closed carriage as they turned into St James's Street, and even more grateful to be able to draw back from the window when they were bowling along Piccadilly, and her mama indicated the Anlaby mansion. Susan, as she risked a glance at the imposing edifice, tried to determine from the tone of voice her mama's feelings towards one of its occupants, Lord John, her erstwhile suitor: but she could discern not the least rancour there, only a perfectly natural interest in the fine residence of a friend.

"There is every likelihood, of course, that you will encounter his lordship in the course of your stay in town," Aurelia went on. "And it will be pleasant for you to see a familiar face, I daresay, amidst all the strange ones."

"Yes, mama," Susan said in a subdued tone, although although her heart was racing: she had not quite realized that meeting him again was so probable — London, she had been telling herself comfortingly, was a big place. Besides which, it was surely in the highest degree unlikely that his lordship, with his famous indifference to young ladies, would go out of his way to meet *her*, the plain, insignificant daughter of the Lydeard Beauty.

However, from that time she was forever looking over her shoulder, and the mere sight of a tall, impressively-built gentleman of aristocratic bearing and impeccable dress was enough to render her pulse tumultuous and her nerves in shreds. As London seemed to be replete with such distingué gentlemen her enjoyment was severely curtailed. Even in the silk warehouse, where the only sign of the opposite sex appeared to be in the person of a young shopman, she could not be wholly at ease, and would have been unsurprised to see Lord John making a critical inspection of the costly bolts of silk for a dressing-gown, perhaps. Indeed, she was completely engrossed in deciding which of the gorgeous brocades on display would best enhance his particular looks, when her mother's voice intruded.

"Really, my dear, if I may not have your attention, I do not know how we are to complete our many purchases," Lady Gillow said, in exasperation, as *she* endeavoured to make up her mind between a Terrendam muslin and a French gauze for a demie-toilette for her daughter — who usually held strong views upon such matters herself. "Perhaps Eleanora was right — we should have had a quiet day resting after yesterday's travelling."

"Oh no! It is merely that I find everything so wonderfully diverting here! Such a bustle and noise everywhere one goes!"

"Yes, of course, London is always a bit overpowering at first. I own I find it so myself after so long in the country."

Susan breathed a sigh of relief as her mama seemed prepared to accept her explanation, and she resolved to put Lord John from her mind, at least until her parent's searching gaze was removed in a few days' time. That she had failed in this endeavour was clear when, on their third morning at Park Place, she was told: "You still do not seem yourself, Susan, and until I can discover what is amiss, I shall feel unwilling to return into Surrey."

The last thing Susan desired was to be under parental scrutiny, if she were to be able to elope successfully: evading Lady Eleanora and Mr Tubb was going to present problems enough, she had decided — in fact, the whole scheme seemed a little ambitious, now that she was actually in London. And, moreover, the continuing absence of the other presumptive eloper, Jermyn, had understandably done nothing to encourage her.

Lady Gillow was straightening the lace ruffled collar, which showed at the throat of her daughter's new rose-coloured pelisse. The two ladies were almost of a height, and Susan did her best not to avert her eyes from the frank, inquiring blue ones of her parent, as she told her yet again there was nothing wrong.

Ignoring this protestation, Aurelia went on thoughtfully: "Is it, I wonder, because Jermyn has not yet returned, and you fear his feelings towards you might have suffered a change? I cannot think your affections were seriously engaged, and yet you did little to discourage his attentions, did you?"

Susan had not foreseen such a direct reference to her cousin, and she was at a loss to know how to respond immediately.

But Aurelia did not wait upon a reply. "I will be perfectly candid with you — Lady Eleanora and I *have* discussed a match between you some time ago, and I own her enthusiasm for it somewhat exceeded mine. But that is not to say I would oppose the connexion if I felt your happiness was at stake. However, I have every reason to suppose you can do a great deal better for yourself, if you wait a while," she emphasised. "You will not, I trust, be influenced by his possession of a fortune — desirable though it may be it is not the whole of marriage. Indeed, I fancy Master Jermyn is capable of running through that in very little time — and I doubt you could exert any check on that tendency," she surmised, with more truth than she knew. Giving a final tweak to a bow at the high-waist of the pelisse, she stood back to survey the result. She nodded her approval and resumed her discourse: "In any event, I am persuaded you will find your sentiments to have been mere infatuation as time goes on. You were thrown a great deal upon each other's company, as you will be again here — and *that* is why I should like to know if I am correct in my supposition?"

Susan was relieved to hear that no insuperable objection seemed to exist to the marriage: it would make it a little easier to elope when the time came. She decided to be as frank as she was able. "I suppose I *am* a little apprehensive at the thought of seeing Jermyn again," she confessed, with a slight smile. "I hope he may not have fixed his interest elsewhere in the meanwhile."

"Well, if he has, and it makes the smallest difference to his attitude to *you*, then you will be fortunate to have made the discovery so soon," Aurelia told her briskly. "But there, if you are utterly convinced he is the parti for you, I hope he may prove to be more constant than that," she continued in kinder, if dubious accents. "All I will say, before I leave the subject, is this — I do beg you will not act hastily. At the moment you stand upon the threshold of your life, and who knows how many offers you may receive before the season is out? Jermyn is not the only man in the world, remember!"

After this disturbing interview, Susan left to go visiting with Lady Eleanora and Camilla, reflecting bitterly to herself that the only man for her loved her mother; and she wondered what she would have said to *that* had she known.

Aurelia stayed for three more days, by which time Jermyn had still not returned to his family, but she was easier in her mind after talking to Susan, and anxious to be at Reibridge again with her own young sons who were home from Harrow.

Susan felt a little guilty at the sense of relief occasioned by her parent's departure, but she was soon in the Tubbs' carriage being conveyed to another shopping orgy in Bond Street, and was allowed scant opportunity to repine.

That evening they dined at home having for once, no engagement for the theatre or a dress-party. Susan was placed next to her host, Mr Berkeley Tubb, an experience she found far from relaxing. This visit had afforded her her first sight of Jermyn's father and, remarking his well-favoured features and lean but impressive bearing, it was easy to see where Jermyn had inherited his handsome looks. (She had quite forgotten her extravagant imaginings about Jermyn's birth now, and scarcely gave the matter a thought: more urgent considerations had supervened).

Mr Tubb, however, for all his attractive appearance was a formidable gentleman, she discovered: his voice was sonorous and his conversational style interrogative. Now that her mama had departed, the full force of his inquisition fell upon her; and they were the sort of questions to which there was no easy answer, and which soon reduced the recipient to a feeling of complete idiocy. ' . . . How do you like Reibridge, Miss Gillow? Tell me about it.' 'You have two young sisters, I collect? Tell me about them'. 'Tell me, what do you find to occupy yourselves in the winter months?' 'Pray tell me, how did Sir Edwin like his university days?' Lady Eleanora's welcome intervention at that point saved her from an admission of total ignorance upon that — to her — almost historical topic: but Susan was quickly approaching the state where the mere sound of that booming voice saying, 'Tell me about it' was sufficient to make her mind an utter blank.

So when Jermyn strolled unannounced into the dining-room, she was doubly overjoyed to see him.

His father apparently was less so.

"What do you mean by interrupting our dinner — and in your travelling dress — when we have been waiting this past week upon your arrival? Come, speak up, sir?"

Jermyn was greeting his mother and sister, but his eager regard had already fixed upon their guest. "I was driven up by a friend in his curricle, sir, thus saving me the price of a place on the Mail," he explained virtuously, whilst exchanging ardent smiles with Susan. "May I sit by you, ma'am?"

But Susan was not allowed a reply before that resonant voice interposed: "You should be banished from the sight of decent company in that full-skirted monstrosity you call a coat! But as we are not entertaining you need not change immediately," Mr Tubb relented. "You may sit this side of your cousin, by me. But do not imagine we are prepared to watch you consume a dozen dishes — no matter how stringent or worthy have been your economies on meals."

Nonetheless, in spite of his father's continuing strictures and remorseless questioning, Jermyn contrived to eat a tolerably good dinner; and also managed to take Susan's hand in an affectionate grip more than once, before the ladies withdrew and abandoned son wholly to father.

"You begin to see what I meant by a certain degree of strife between them?" Camilla whispered in Susan's ear as they made their way to the drawing-room. "I own I have been dreading his return."

But Susan thought this parental discord might at least prevent brother and sister bickering all the while, and so it proved. In fact she saw Jermyn in a much better light than hitherto: away from his father he was all good-nature, and absence, she decided, had certainly made his heart grow fonder towards her. Had she wished to avoid his attentions, it would have been very difficult to do so in a house which was strange to her, but she did not: consequently, as no attempt was ever made to chaperon them, they spent a good deal of time alone together.

In view of this circumstance she was relieved that his conduct was altogether more restrained than it had been at Reibridge, and, beyond taking up her hand occasionally and placing a kiss rather abstractedly upon it, he spent the greater part of his time in earnest conversation. He laid the blame for most of his present discontent firmly at the door of his father; and with this Susan could hardly fail to sympathize, as she was a constant witness to Mr Tubb's overbearing ways.

"You see m'father has this maggoty notion in his head that I am born to be an ornament of the legal profession," Jermyn said in confiding tones, when he had been home a week — although he had told her of this before during one of their many *tête-a-têtes*. "Oh, I know what lies at the root of it! He was an actor in his salad days, you know, and is fearful I shall sink as low as he. As if I *would*!" he exclaimed indignantly. "Mixing with ill-bred fellows of that sort." He shuddered, and draped a languid hand over the high curve of the sofa.

The last item of family history Jermyn had not mentioned before, and it took Susan's interest at once: so that was why Mr Tubb had such an oratorical style to

286

his speech, she thought.

"But I have no more inclination to strut about in a court speechifying, than on a stage," Jermyn continued his protest, with some energy.

"What would you like to do?" Susan asked.

He looked quite affronted. "I don't need to *do* anything! Dash it all — I've no wish to sound insufferable, but I'm as plump in the pocket as need be, and am not likely to want for a roll of soft until I stick my spoon in the wall! It was always different for m'father — never had a sixpence to scratch with when he married."

Susan looked very impressed. "Your father must have done exceedingly well since — I had no idea that being an attorney was so advantageous." She was thinking of Edwin's future prospects, in part.

For a moment Jermyn stared at her. "No, no, you misunderstand — *my* inheritance comes from m'mother's family. Father has done tolerably well," he said condescendingly, and waving an arm at the stylish furnishings about them. "But

I fear he has not much overplus, even now ... And that's another reason I want to quit Oxford," he declared, with an apparent non-sequitur.

"I'm sorry — ?" Susan murmured, frowning.

"Oh — well, you see the case is this — I have had an allowance from the trust of a thousand a year since I was eighteen — which ain't very long," he interpolated feelingly. "And no sooner do I get it, than I'm entered for Oxford, and that costs not a penny less than six hundred pounds a year, merely to maintain a creditable appearance — which leaves me with a paltry four hundred pounds for *everything else*," he emphasized gloomily. "M'father can't stand the huff, you see, so it has to come out of my allowance. Which is all very fine, if I had the smallest inclination or reason to be there in the first place."

"Yes, it does seem rather a waste," Susan agreed cautiously, and thinking she detected a possible opening here, perhaps, for her own plan for their future.

"Waste! It's a monstrous imposition,

and I'm dashed if I'll tolerate it! My allowance for this quarter has gone already, and here am I with my pockets to let, when I should be as rich as Croesus — relatively speaking." he concluded with a sudden surge of modesty.

"But what can you do about it?" Susan saw to her surprise that this simple question had a powerful effect upon her audience: the easy, confidential manner evaporated; he twitched nervously at his cravat, cleared his throat once or twice, and looked almost as abashed as on the occasion when Lord John had disturbed him in the library.

"The truth is," he began tentatively, "there's precious little I *can* do on my own . . . But, if I were to marry," he went on, avoiding her gaze, "that would be something quite else."

"Oh? And how is that?" she prompted him, in the most abominably ingenuous fashion, for which she instantly despised herself.

"I am to have full control of my fortune bestowed upon me with marriage — at *whatever age*," he asserted. "Of course m'mother holds the reins of the trust, so it has to be someone who meets with her approval." Here he permitted himself a speculative look at his cousin. "Frankly I had rather be riveted," he went on, fixing her now with a steady gaze, "than spend the next few years painfully acquiring a reputation for the most nip-farthing fellow at Oxford." He grinned. "I may add that even *I* do not fear being designated the most buffle-headed — there is spirited competition for that honour!" After a brief pause he went on in more sombre tones: "There *is* one other alternative open to me, and one which some of my friends have little choice but to follow — there are money-lenders in the city only too willing to — "

"*No!*" cried Susan, startling her companion with her vehemence. "I am persuaded that that would be foolish beyond permission, more particularly when you are in no way impoverished, or compelled to seek their aid." Her pretty cornflower eyes were round with alarm as she pictured Jermyn upon the same road to ruin as Edwin. "The interest those gentlemen charge is stupefyingly large

— or so I believe," she qualified hastily, seeing the interested look she had drawn upon herself.

"By Jove, for a moment you sounded just like my pater!" he gasped. "But you are right, of course, and your sentiments wholly accord with my own on the matter, I am delighted to hear," he said in a voice redolent with meaning; but nonetheless Susan looked in vain for any impulsive proposal.

Sensing that no better opportunity was likely to come her way for the furtherance of her scheme — indeed, she had never dreamed it would be so simple — she decided to take the plunge, and throw out a quite appallingly brazen hint.

"If there were to be a match between your family and my own," she said slowly, feeling her way with the utmost care, and very watchful of his expression, "I have reason to suppose it would not be met by any parental opposition."

He gave no sign of immediate rejoicing beyond a businesslike grunt; then said at last: "*Your* parent maybe, but what of mine?"

She pressed her lips together nervously,

and nodded. "Yours as well, I collect," she confirmed; although if she were honest, she reflected guiltily, she should have excluded Mr Tubb.

"By Jupiter, you're a regular sly-boots and no mistake!" he exclaimed in obvious admiration, and slapping his tightly pantalooned knees. "I'm dashed if I know how you discovered that, but never mind!" He got to his feet abruptly, and stood looking out of the tall window — which, as it overlooked a cul-de-sac, offered no distractions to his racing thoughts. Outwardly he looked quite calm, elbow supported by hand, finger across lips, so Susan was taken completely unawares when he spun round with a: "So! There's no need to delay, is there? In my view we may elope any time."

"*Elope?*" she echoed, with just as much astonishment and outrage as if the thought of such a thing had never before crossed her mind. Indeed, in spite of everything, she did now entertain the greatest misgivings on the subject: consenting to their marriage was one thing, but bestowing their blessing and a fortune upon an eloping couple was surely another? she had realized belatedly. She said as much to Jermyn.

"Ah, but you see there I am in an unusually powerful position," he replied with a smug smile. "For my parents, you must know, eloped themselves, and caused the devil of an uproar, so they could scarcely nab the rust if I were to do the same, could they? Stands to reason — they'd not want to spread it abroad. So, if I were to disappear for a few days north of the border, and come back leg-shackled, the best thing they could do is accept the *fait accompli* with a good grace. In fact, I wouldn't be surprised if they didn't insist upon a fashionable wedding at once — so, if you like that sort of frippery affair, it would not be denied you," he said, showing a sudden if disparaging interest in Susan's point of view. "Yes, they'll keep mum about an elopement — I'd wager my fortune upon it! Well — I suppose I will be, in a way!" He laughed then a trifle uncertainly.

Susan was struck dumb by these revelations: in one short speech she had discovered Lady Eleanora's secret past — and had her own future sealed.

# 15

AFTER Jermyn's astonishing disclosures, Susan made a supreme effort and recovered her power of speech eventually; but all she could utter was a very pertinent, if unromantic question. "How — how much is your fortune, if I may ask?" For if it were not substantial enough to withstand twenty-five thousand pounds being clipped off it without making any material difference, there was no real reason for her to be carried along any further by these rather incredible events. In truth her resolution was beginning to fail her, and she found herself hoping desperately it had been grossly exaggerated.

At this further evidence of his wife to-be's financial acumen and interest, Jermyn gave her a slightly startled look. "Two hundred thousand pounds, soundly invested, which — as I am sure you must know," he added ironically, "will bring me an income of ten thousand pounds a year."

"I see," she said faintly, too overset to notice the tone of his voice. That was wealth beyond her imagining, and she could not reasonably tell herself it was insufficient — a dozen brilliant seasons would probably not throw a richer husband in her way. As she did not any longer anticipate marrying for love, this must represent an offer she could ill-afford to reject . . .

"You do understand why I should find several years of poverty irksome?" Jermyn was saying.

"Oh, indeed! A truly monstrous prospect!" she agreed, whilst wondering how to put her final — but vital — question to him. She began by saying humbly: "My portion, of course, can in no way match your inheritance. I believe it to be a trifling ten thousand pounds, and at the moment I am in possession of an allowance of a few hundreds."

He waved his hand impatiently. "That does not signify. You would not find me ungenerous, for above everything I should want a wife of whom I could be proud, and always dressed in the first style of elegance. Yes, you would certainly need a completely new wardrobe of clothes," he said, casting a despairing glance at her recently-acquired morning-dress of best white Nainsook, lavishly trimmed with blonde lace fichu and flounces, and of which she was sneakingly quite proud.

However, this was no time to stand upon one's dignity — rather she had to grovel, an attitude which did not come naturally to one of her independent character. "Oh, yes," she acknowledged, swallowing her principles, "you are right! I am a complete dowd and would need *everything* new. I have very expensive tastes, too, I may say, so it would be a costly affair," she said threateningly; but to make a bald demand for twenty-five thousand pounds was, she discovered, quite beyond her powers. How ever lavish her expenditure on clothes it could not equal that sum, and in any event she would not be likely to handle the money: Jermyn would simply pay the bills.

Then, in her hour of need, a brilliant idea came to her which might just serve the trick, she thought. Giving herself no time for reflection, she grasped the nettle. "I do consider, and feel sure you must agree, that the true lady of fashion needs the very best jewellery to adorn her person. When one is young, of course, diamonds are the only stones one may wear if one is to have any claim to elegance." Fearing that her audience, who was regarding her with a fascinated eye, might interrupt, she hurried on rather breathlessly: "A parure — of matching stones of the first water — would suffice. Necklace . . . tiara . . . brooch . . . bracelet . . . ear-rings," she enumerated, in case he should not know what she considered comprised a respectable parure. "Oh — and a ring, of course. That would also solve the difficulty of a bride present, would it not?" she concluded with a helpful air.

"Admirably — if I were heir to the mines of Golconda," he said in a shaken under-voice, and with a rather glazed expression upon his face. "Such a set of gems would cost a fortune, you know," he pointed out, recovering a little, but not realizing that that was the whole purpose of the suggestion; as the happy bride had hopes of raising at least twenty-five thousand pounds in a trice by having paste copies made at once and selling, or perhaps pawning (at the moment she scarcely knew which) the originals. "Besides," he further elaborated, causing panic in his listener "to be bedecked in jewels is very outré, and far from modish."

"But diamonds can *never* be outré," she declared firmly, before all was lost. "After all, Princess Charlotte was *covered* in them at her wedding," she said, with what she hoped was an irrefutable argument.

"Maybe — but I think you'll find them somewhat *de trop* at Gretna Green," he said drily, whilst he consulted his fob watch. "You must excuse me now, I have to change."

"Are you accompanying us to the theatre tonight?" Susan asked, relieved their discussion was over for the moment.

"No, I fear not. I had a previous engagement," he told her rather stiffly, and took his leave.

Susan sat alone for a time, her emotions in considerable turmoil. When

Camilla joined her fifteen minutes later, she had, by going over her recent unfortunate conversation, reached the disturbing conclusion that an elopement was likely, but a parure of diamonds was not. However, she thought, determined to make the best of a situation which was largely her own doing, she could probably contrive *some* scheme to extract money from Jermyn after they were wed: she did not think that at heart his was an ungenerous nature. The truth was, his enthusiasm for elopement had come as a prodigious surprise; deep down she had never really thought he would consider it.

Susan was glad that the evening's entertainment was an undemanding visit to Drury Lane theatre; and she was tolerably sure that Lord John would not be encountered there, as he must still be in mourning for his brother, judging by her own experience when her father died. This circumstance also precluded seeing him at anything but the smaller gatherings. All in all she was beginning to think her mama had exaggerated the chances of their meeting.

Not knowing when she was going to be called upon to elope was discomposing, and Susan began to acquire a reputation for vagueness and lack of interest in her partners which quite exasperated her chaperon and hostess, Lady Eleanora: who, if she had known what lay at the root of it, would have been quite horrified — it was, after all, her worst fear coming to fruition.

Since Jermyn had proposed (and that, although it had fallen short of her expectations in many ways, was how Susan regarded their rather odd exchange) their moments alone, once rather frequent, had dwindled to nothing. However, this was not hard to explain, as the pace of the season was increasing and scarcely a minute passed without a new invitation arriving or an outing being arranged — and Jermyn, bent upon his own diversions, was scarcely ever at home. The only respite Susan had from the hectic round of visits and entertainments was occasionally when Lady Eleanora received her morning-callers alone: however if there were young people in the party, the girls would also be expected to be in attendance.

About a week after Susan's unsettling interview with Jermyn, just such a circumstance arose; Camilla and she were sprawling in most unladylike attitudes in the little music-room, feeling very jaded after an excessively late night, when the footman informed them her ladyship required their presence in the drawing-room.

After a degree of good-natured complaining, and a cursory tidying of their hair and smoothing of muslin, the two young ladies went on their way prepared to entertain their guests.

But there was only one visitor standing by Lady Eleanora's side: and Susan almost turned upon her heel when she saw who that 'one' was.

Lord John's garb was of unrelieved black — coat, waistcoat and pantaloons — which threw into sharp contrast the dazzling white of his linen; he still contrived to make every other gentleman she had seen look perfunctory in his dress, she thought — even in town. But her thoughts did not dwell upon his clothes for more than a fleeting moment: why had he called? she wondered, in the greatest agitation. It was true he was acquainted with Lady Eleanora, and there was no reason why he should not call upon her family: and excluding their house-guest might look a trifle odd, she told herself in a calming fashion.

So, by the time the greetings were over, she had convinced herself that his visit was nothing more than a social call from an acquaintance and neighbour. Observing him as closely as her shyness would allow, she came to the conclusion *he* was a trifle less assured in his mien than before, and seemed to be as unwilling to encounter her eye as she was to meet his. When she considered this, she had to admit he had every reason to view her a shade warily: her half-brother owed him a fortune; and her mother — whom he loved — was, for whatever reason, about to wed another. Added to which was his recent family tragedy of losing an only brother — small wonder then, if he seemed to display less than his customary suavity and flow of spirits.

The conversation was innocuous, and maintained with the utmost skill by Lady

Eleanora; Camilla and Susan taking little part, and Lord John evidently content to follow his hostess's lead as they discussed mutual friends, current theatrical offerings (which his lordship had not seen), and finally, the recent attack upon the Prince Regent's carriage by a mob in the Park (which his lordship had happened to witness). This last topic could have led to a lengthy political discourse on the unrest abroad in the country amongst the reformers, but Lady Eleanora chose that moment to rise.

"My dear," she said, pointedly addressing her daughter, "I think we must excuse ourselves from this pleasant gathering — I need your help in putting the finishing touches to our arrangements for the rout-party."

Susan was interested to see that her cousin's bewilderment, as she made to follow her mother, equalled her own: Lady Eleanora was clearly indulging in a subterfuge to leave her with Lord John, as they had no party fixed for that evening. She hoped she could depend upon his usual facility with words, for she knew herself to be quite incapable of uttering a sound at that moment: mercifully her anxieties upon that head were short-lived.

"Forgive me for having to resort to such clumsy stratagems, but I must talk with you, and beneath Lady Eleanora's roof seemed to offer the most conformable way to contrive a private meeting — and her ladyship has been everything that is obliging."

Susan was passing under rapid mental review the subjects they could have in common: her mama was the prime one, but he would scarcely discuss that affair with her, *surely*? Edwin was the next who came to mind, but she was sworn to secrecy upon that head. The only other item which darted into her perplexed brain was: "*Glenarvon!*" she exclaimed, without further thought. "You want it back, to be sure, and it is very remiss of me, I know, but I have left it — " There she broke off, startled by Lord John's laughter.

"My dear girl!" he cried, greatly amused. "I would scarcely go to such lengths to repossess a *book*! — Pray forgive me," he went on, in more sober tones, "I have placed you at a disadvantage, and you must believe me, I have not the smallest wish to discomfit you . . . But, to tell the truth, I feel a trifle discomfited myself, and perhaps you will be good enough to bear with me for a moment?" He sat back, fingers interlaced over the funereal waistcoat, and surveyed her somewhat ruefully. "I believe when first we met you judged me to be bold, and long past the age of embarrassment. That, I can tell you now, is certainly not so."

Susan was quite unnerved by this new, subdued Lord John, and as she had no notion still which members of her family, or what mutual topic he wished to discuss, she kept silent.

"I have wanted to speak long before now, I may say, but events appear to have conspired against me. Having at least been given this opportunity — well, I will digress no more . . . Simply, Miss Gillow, I have come to ask if you will marry me?"

He had supposed any young lady would be thrown into a degree of confusion upon receiving a proposal of marriage;

but Miss Gillow's rapid change of colour, startled looks and continuing silence did not, he fancied, bode well for him. And so it proved.

"You wish to marry *me*?" Susan echoed finally, placing a curious emphasis on the last word.

"Are you so surprised that I should so wish?"

"Of course I am!" she burst out immoderately, as she tried to restore some order to her chaotic thoughts. Then she began to see what might have happened: he could not wed her mother because of the need to produce an heir, but if he were to marry *her* that difficulty would be overcome — *and* he would still be fulfilling the conditions agreed for absolving Edwin from his crippling debt. Why his lordship should go to such excessive lengths to accomplish that, was quite beyond her. But could Edwin, perhaps, have had some hand in it? she thought wildly. Hadn't he said something of the sort to her once, about marrying a fortune? "Well, *really*!" she fulminated, before pausing to reflect what utter nonsense that must be, and before her unhappy suitor could begin to explain. Then she demanded abruptly: "Have you seen my step-brother recently?"

Clearly relieved at the impersonal nature of the question, he said meekly: "I have indeed had that pleasure, when I rode into Surrey earlier in the week to see your mother."

"My *mother*?" Susan repeated, sounding aghast, and becoming more confused every minute that went by. "You know, I suppose, that she is to marry again very soon?" She was determined to clear up one mystery at least.

"Why yes," he responded, puzzled, then added; "It is customary you know to consult the parent of one's intended bride."

Susan was astounded by his cool effrontery in treating this as a *perfectly ordinary* proposal, when she was clearly being used as a pawn in some deep game. If only he *had* fallen in love with her, instead of her mother! But on these terms she could never marry him: she had as lief elope with Jermyn as they had planned; indeed, as far as she was concerned, her word had been given to her cousin and she would not go back on that. With that arrangement she was helping Edwin, eventually, and enabling Jermyn to come into possession of his fortune: she would not let him down. Oh, but if only things had worked out differently! she thought with sudden anguish.

These painful reflections were easily discernible in her expressive eyes, and Lord John leaned forward. "Look, I do not pretend to know why my humble proposal has so overset you," he began earnestly. "Nor why it should surprise you that I dare to offer for your hand — unless," he hesitated, "you consider me a good deal too old for you?"

The hurt in his eyes was such that Susan at once went to great pains to reassure him on that account. He was still bent forward, his elbow resting upon his knees, and he was examining a perfectly manicured finger-nail with apparent displeasure. "Well then, why is it you find me so repulsive?" he asked, and in such saddened tones that Susan had the greatest urge to fling her arms about him, and tell him that far from finding him repulsive she loved him to distraction. But she soon reminded herself of his inexplicable behaviour in transferring his attentions from her mother so blithely, and of her own commitment to Jermyn.

So, she sat there very sedately, with her hands folded in her lap and, with her gaze fixed upon that dear, dark head, she said in a failing voice: "No, no, of course I don't find you repulsive — how absurd of you to say so."

He looked up then, and the expression in those disturbingly attractive brown eyes was such that she blinked and turned away. "Perhaps, then, you consider yourself promised elsewhere?"

This shaft was so accurate she could only nod, and pray that would mark the end of the appallingly uncomfortable encounter. Jermyn, she knew, would be returning soon from a morning spent at Tattersall's, and he might, even now, have made arrangements for their flight. He had had another skirmish with his father at breakfast, and knowing he was exceedingly impulsive, she lived in constant expectation of a whispered instruction that she must instantly pack her portmanteau for Scotland . . .

"In that event, it does not take extraordinary powers of deduction," Lord John was saying, "to imagine the gentleman's identity — but I must own I am sadly disappointed. I did my best to hint you away before: he is not worthy of you, you must know that. I told you — so many moons ago — not to be deceived by fine feathers and mere romantic good looks."

Susan, by this time exceedingly edgy, and only anxious to escape, threw caution to the winds and said caustically: "It ill-becomes you, my lord, to criticize someone behind his back *and* under his own roof. Yes, I do recall your interfering ways," she went on, fully launched now and scarcely aware of what she was saying. "But at that time I daresay you felt encouraged to speak by the thought that you would soon be my step-father. Well, you are not!"

"Your *what?*" ejaculated her dumb-founded listener.

"Oh, I expect you will deny it, but there is really no point in your doing so," she declared, determined now to brazen it out, although she knew she should never have alluded to such a delicate matter. "I have, you see, been in Edwin's *complete* confidence, ever since he returned to Reibridge and had his meeting with you," she said darkly.

Lord John looked even more thunderstruck. "The devil you were," he muttered.

"Yes, so you see there can be nothing further to discuss between us." She rose to her feet, and smoothed the gauzy blue folds of her gown. "Depend upon it, my lord, the Gillows shall not stand indebted to you for very much longer," she told him, in what was intended for a dignified parting shot.

But he countered at once, with profound feeling: "No, by God, they will not! Sit down, ma'am!" he commanded, and Susan recognized the tone of voice from the day he had brought back Jermyn injured from the hunting-field: he expected to be obeyed and he was. She sat down. "Now," he said firmly, "you have some explaining to do, I think."

"Indeed I have not!" retorted Susan. "*You* are the *one* to explain your extraordinary conduct — if you can!"

Loftily ignoring this gibe, he asked: "Where, in heaven's name, did you pitch upon this hare-brained notion that I was to wed Lady Gillow?"

It was Susan's turn to be confounded. "But everyone said you would, and *you told* Edwin you had every intention of doing so. Oh, I know you thought it to be very secret, but it was not."

Lord John ran a hand distractedly through his hair, which he had taken particular pains with that morning, and tried to recall what had passed between Sir Edwin and himself to cause this disastrous misunderstanding. "I am not often at a loss for words but I fear I am dangerously near it at the moment." He took a deep breath. "Will you please believe me when I say that, whatever anyone may have expected, *I* never had the least intention of marrying your mama, delightful lady and exceptional beauty though she is. Indeed, it was perfectly clear to me, almost from the beginning, that Sir Anthony would have shown me short shrift if I had even attempted to cut him out. You must have been unobservant to a degree, because

I am tolerably sure Mrs Selworthy, for one, was also fully aware of Sir Anthony's aspirations. I heard her hint as much upon one occasion — although, unlike some, I set little store by such gossip."

Susan was about to dispute the point, but when she thought about it she could not, at this distance, recall her aunt's precise words: in any event, there was a more important matter to settle. "Your agreement with Edwin, then, was all a hum, merely to allay his fears about his debt to you for the time being? Was not that a rather cruel and bizarre joke?"

"Abominably so, if you were right," he conceded. "It was *not* a hum — and indeed you must have a peculiar notion of your fellow beings' behaviour to entertain the idea for a moment — which must stem from your avid novel reading, I fancy," he said in passing. "But, to return to the point, it was a monstrously unfortunate case of misunderstanding and false impressions, caused by my misguided insistence upon secrecy. I could not understand at the time how Edwin came to be privy to my intentions towards you: but I naturally presumed

Lady Gillow, whom I consulted first — when I sought her permission to lend you *Glenarvon*, incidentally — had told him. Lord, I was a fool! I should not have waited until now to declare myself." He gave an odd little laugh. "You see, I was so anxious you should be uninfluenced by anyone but myself — and look where it has brought me!"

Susan had been staring at him in stupefaction for some time. "Do you mean to say that all along it was *I* — ?"

"Well, of course it was, you little gudgeon! You would have known if you had not been so determined — for lord knows what reason — to pair me off with your mama! And had had eyes for anyone but that jackanapes — I know! I must not abuse him under his own roof! But he has tried me sorely for months, and I feel entitled to protest a little at this juncture!"

As the whole story began to fall into place, Susan did not know whether to laugh or cry: all she had had to do was wait for Lord John to propose. Edwin would have been solvent again, and together with his plans to take up the law, would almost certainly have been united with his Catherine by this time. If only her own head had not been filled with bookish romantic ideas about handsome heroes — Lord John was right on that count . . .

"You cannot be so misguided as to marry him, I do not believe it," he stated flatly.

"But I have given him my word," she said, in tones of abject misery. Indeed, she thought to her shame, had virtually proposed to him herself . . .

"If I may say so, the prospect does not appear to afford you any great joy." She offered no reply to this, and he went on, almost as if talking to himself: "It seems just a trifle odd that Lady Eleanora should be unaware of this impending marriage, and she would surely have thought it proper to have mentioned it when I spoke to her earlier? And your parent, although she had just left you here, also seemed to be in a state of blissful ignorance — although she did have some misgivings in that quarter, I collect. So," he continued his soliloquy, "it is not an arranged marriage, which must leave us with a love match. Now, I would beg leave to doubt that Mr Tubb is capable of loving anyone but himself for the moment — later perhaps, although I would not count upon it, even then."

Susan was squirming under this examination, and was quite unable to meet her companion's eyes, although he was scarcely a couple of yards away. Consequently, she still managed to be surprised when he reached across and took her hand in his.

" — And you, I am persuaded, feel no ungovernable passion for your cousin. So what lies at the root of this marriage of yours, I know not. Some devious scheme of Master Tubb's, I'll warrant . . . Look at me," he entreated, for although she had not withdrawn her hands from his grasp, she still avoided his gaze. But she swallowed rather lumpily, and obeyed him. "What I do know, you odd little creature, is that *I love you*, and although I have to own that my feeble attempts to win your respect have constantly foundered, I will not allow that greenhorn to carry you off without a fight . . . Now, let us suppose you did *not* feel yourself committed to someone else, would you then consider my offer?" he asked gently.

She nodded, quite bereft of speech, and then snatched her hands away and burst into tears.

"Do you know, I had no notion proposing was so wearing," he remarked, as the brief storm subsided. "It makes me thankful I have not attempted it before — one has to be very sure it is worth it." But he was smiling, and it would have taken a harder heart than Susan's to have resisted that smile: she even managed a watery one in return.

"That's better . . . Now, may I take it that my offer has been accepted?" he asked patiently.

She gave a final sniff into her handkerchief, and said: "Yes, thank you, and I'm sorry to have been so . . . foolish." It sounded appallingly inadequate to her own ears — Lord knew how it seemed to him. "But what am I to do about Mr Tubb?"

"Tell him you have changed your mind — that's a woman's privilege, is it not?"

her suitor said smoothly.

Visions of an outraged Jermyn, deprived of his fortune and his immediate escape from University, swam before her eyes, and she did not know how she was to face it — but she would, she told herself grimly. She only hoped he had not completed the arrangements for their journey north.

"Yes, I will," she said in staunch tones, and as she looked adoringly at Lord John she felt she would have the strength to face any adversity now. But she had behaved so *badly* towards him, and so blindly, she thought in another spasm of guilt: so she resolved to make up for her lamentable conduct without more ado. "I daresay you will not believe me," she said in a low, shy voice, "but I do love you as well — have done so for — oh, a long time!"

"Oh yes, I believe you," he declared, with what seemed to her to be amazing perspicacity. "I would scarcely have felt so confident about waiting until now to propose if I had thought you *quite* indifferent. But I must own you gave me a sad fright earlier."

"I know — I'm sorry!" she said again, and this time she did yield to impulse and stretched out her hands towards him. It was the moment he had been so patiently awaiting, and he drew her to him without hesitation: so she found herself blissfully enfolded in his arms — something she had scarcely ever dared to dream about.

After a few moments the door was flung open, and Jermyn said: "Mama? Look whom I met in the Park! — Oh — Well, I'm dashed!" He stood there surveying the scene in his long, many-caped driving-coat, and his gloves still in his hand; and immediately behind him could be discerned a lady in the shadows.

Susan would have leapt to her feet, as she had done so long ago in the library at home, but her captor restrained her, and addressed the new arrival with great affability: "Ah, Mr Tubb, as you see, you have the immense satisfaction of turning the tables upon me." He released Susan, and then stood up himself. "However, before you attribute any impropriety to the proceedings, I would like you to know that Miss Gillow and I are to be wed."

Susan stiffened upon hearing this, and waited in acute apprehension for Jermyn to lash himself into a fury, feeling convinced that the presence of the lady, whose face she could not see clearly beneath the bonnet, would exercise no curb upon his turbulent nature. But to her amazement her cousin merely watched them silently for a time, and then a slow smile broke over his face.

"Are you, by Jove?" he drawled. "Well, my lord, if you take my advice you will look to your pocket-book, and lock up the family jewels forthwith — that's a deucedly expensive lady you have there! She will take you sailing down the river Tick before the honeymoon is over, mark my words." After delivering this blighting judgement, he turned and drew his interested companion — now seen to be a red-head of ample proportions — into the room.

Bestowing a besotted smile upon her, he said: "You both know Miss Etheridge, of course."

Susan took her hand in a kind of happy stupor. 'And so shall Gretna Green . . . ' she thought mischievously.

## THE END

*Other titles in the*
*Ulverscroft Large Print Series:*

## TO FIGHT THE WILD
### Rod Ansell and Rachel Percy

Lost in uncharted Australian bush, Rod Ansell survived by hunting and trapping wild animals, improvising shelter and using all the bushman's skills he knew.

## COROMANDEL
### Pat Barr

India in the 1830s is a hot, uncomfortable place, where the East India Company still rules. Amelia and her new husband find themselves caught up in the animosities which seethe between the old order and the new.

## THE SMALL PARTY
### Lillian Beckwith

A frightening journey to safety begins for Ruth and her small party as their island is caught up in the dangers of armed insurrection.

## THE WILDERNESS WALK
### Sheila Bishop

Stifling unpleasant memories of a misbegotten romance in Cleave with Lord Francis Aubrey, Lavinia goes on holiday there with her sister. The two women are thrust into a romantic intrigue involving none other than Lord Francis.

## THE RELUCTANT GUEST
### Rosalind Brett

Ann Calvert went to spend a month on a South African farm with Theo Borland and his sister. They both proved to be different from her first idea of them, and there was Storr Peterson — the most disturbing man she had ever met.

## ONE ENCHANTED SUMMER
### Anne Tedlock Brooks

A tale of mystery and romance and a girl who found both during one enchanted summer.

## CLOUD OVER MALVERTON
### Nancy Buckingham

Dulcie soon realises that something is seriously wrong at Malverton, and when violence strikes she is horrified to find herself under suspicion of murder.


## AFTER THOUGHTS
### Max Bygraves

The Cockney entertainer tells stories of his East End childhood, of his RAF days, and his post-war showbusiness successes and friendships with fellow comedians.


## MOONLIGHT
## AND MARCH ROSES
### D. Y. Cameron

Lynn's search to trace a missing girl takes her to Spain, where she meets Clive Hendon. While untangling the situation, she untangles her emotions and decides on her own future.

## NURSE ALICE IN LOVE
### Theresa Charles

Accepting the post of nurse to little Fernie Sherrod, Alice Everton could not guess at the romance, suspense and danger which lay ahead at the Sherrod's isolated estate.


## POIROT INVESTIGATES
### Agatha Christie

Two things bind these eleven stories together — the brilliance and uncanny skill of the diminutive Belgian detective, and the stupidity of his Watson-like partner, Captain Hastings.


## LET LOOSE THE TIGERS
### Josephine Cox

Queenie promised to find the long-lost son of the frail, elderly murderess, Hannah Jason. But her enquiries threatened to unlock the cage where crucial secrets had long been held captive.

## THE TWILIGHT MAN
### Frank Gruber

Jim Rand lives alone in the California desert awaiting death. Into his hermit existence comes a teenage girl who blows both his past and his brief future wide open.

## DOG IN THE DARK
### Gerald Hammond

Jim Cunningham breeds and trains gun dogs, and his antagonism towards the devotees of show spaniels earns him many enemies. So when one of them is found murdered, the police are on his doorstep within hours.

## THE RED KNIGHT
### Geoffrey Moxon

When he finds himself a pawn on the chessboard of international espionage with his family in constant danger, Guy Trent becomes embroiled in moves and countermoves which may mean life or death for Western scientists.

## TIGER TIGER
### Frank Ryan

A young man involved in drugs is found murdered. This is the first event which will draw Detective Inspector Sandy Woodings into a whirlpool of murder and deceit.

## CAROLINE MINUSCULE
### Andrew Taylor

Caroline Minuscule, a medieval script, is the first clue to the whereabouts of a cache of diamonds. The search becomes a deadly kind of fairy story in which several murders have an other-worldly quality.

## LONG CHAIN OF DEATH
### Sarah Wolf

During the Second World War four American teenagers from the same town join the Army together. Forty-two years later, the son of one of the soldiers realises that someone is systematically wiping out the families of the four men.

## THE LISTERDALE MYSTERY
### Agatha Christie

Twelve short stories ranging from the light-hearted to the macabre, diverse mysteries ingeniously and plausibly contrived and convincingly unravelled.

## TO BE LOVED
### Lynne Collins

Andrew married the woman he had always loved despite the knowledge that Sarah married him for reasons of her own. So much heartache could have been avoided if only he had known how vital it was to be loved.

## ACCUSED NURSE
### Jane Converse

Paula found herself accused of a crime which could cost her her job, her nurse's reputation, and even the man she loved, unless the truth came to light.

## BUTTERFLY MONTANE
### Dorothy Cork

Parma had come to New Guinea to marry Alec Rivers, but she found him completely disinterested and that overbearing Pierce Adams getting entirely the wrong idea about her.


## HONOURABLE FRIENDS
### Janet Daley

Priscilla Burford is happily married when she meets Junior Environment Minister Alistair Thurston. Inevitably, sexual obsession and political necessity collide.


## WANDERING MINSTRELS
### Mary Delorme

Stella Wade's career as a concert pianist might have been ruined by the rudeness of a famous conductor, so it seemed to her agent and benefactor. Even Sir Nicholas fails to see the possibilities when John Tallis falls deeply in love with Stella.

## MORNING IS BREAKING
### Lesley Denny

The growing frenzy of war catapults Diane Clements into a clandestine marriage and separation with a German refugee.


## LAST BUS TO WOODSTOCK
### Colin Dexter

A girl's body is discovered huddled in the courtyard of a Woodstock pub, and Detective Chief Inspector Morse and Sergeant Lewis are hunting a rapist and a murderer.


## THE STUBBORN TIDE
### Anne Durham

Everyone advised Carol not to grieve so excessively over her cousin's death. She might have followed their advice if the man she loved thought that way about her, but another girl came first in his affections.